THE BEAUTIFUL GOLDEN FRAME

Millionaire Bernard Rivers hired a private detective when a vengeful madwoman threatened to burn down his magnificent home. Rivers didn't care about his house but he did care about the picture inside, for it was the sole reminder of his beautiful wife, Judith, killed two years before under strange circumstances. Fire was the only real threat to the picture, but Mark Preston, Private Eye, knew that stopping a mad aggressor with a flaming torch was almost impossible . . .

PETER CHAMBERS

◆

THE BEAUTIFUL GOLDEN FRAME

LINFORD
Leicester

First published in Great Britain in 1980

First Linford Edition
published 2003

The characters and situations in this book are
entirely imaginary and bear no relation to any
real person or actual happening

British Library CIP Data

Chambers, Peter, *1924 –*
    The beautiful golden frame.
    —Large print ed.—
    Linford mystery library
    1. Detective and mystery stories
    2. Large type books
    I. Title
    823.9'14 [F]

    ISBN 0–7089–4852–9

Published by
F. A. Thorpe (Publishing)
Anstey, Leicestershire

Set by Words & Graphics Ltd.
Anstey, Leicestershire
Printed and bound in Great Britain by
T. J. International Ltd., Padstow, Cornwall

This book is printed on acid-free paper

It's only a beautiful picture
In a beautiful golden frame.

Old Music-Hall Song

1

The house happened quite suddenly. The road took a curving bend to the left, between rolling, parched hills. And there it was, snuggled securely into the side of a gentle slope. The architect knew his California, and had neatly avoided the usual transplanted Kentucky, or early Hollywood. Instead he'd gone back over the years to the original Spanish influence, picking up points from the scattered monasteries, the occasional hacienda, and utilising the most attractive features he found. The result was Rivers Bend, a white and sparkling building which seemed to blend with the landscape, rather than impose on it. There wasn't any river. The name had been given to the house by its owner, the man I'd come to see, Bernard L. Rivers.

As I parked the car at the foot of a flight of stone stairs, I knew one thing about Mr Rivers. He kept a neat establishment. The rolling lawns were immaculate, with regularly-spaced bushes planted in strict order. Even the colours of the flowers were scattered mathematically, forming a pattern. A low white fountain made a soft shushing noise, catching the sun a million ways as it dropped gently onto a large fish pond. I didn't look at the fish. There would certainly be two of each size and colour, and they probably swam in Busby Berkeley patterns.

I'd seen the girl as I got out of the car. She wasn't hard to spot. She was perched on one corner of the stone balustrade that ran the length of the house. That way, the slim brown figure was silhouetted against the sky. So that there was no possibility I might miss anything, she was combing her hair, an activity which required her to hold her head back. Both arms were behind her head as she took long careful strokes at the gleaming honey-coloured hair. This naturally required her to arch her back, so that the slim pointed breasts jutted out, accentuating the flat tightness of the rest of her. Although I passed within twenty feet, she pretended not to notice me. The least I could do was return the compliment.

The front door stood open, and the interior looked cool. I stared around for something to press or bang.

'Hi.'

The speaker was a young man in his early twenties. He was tall, crew-cut, good-looking. He wore a dirty sweatshirt, and a pair of jeans cut off ragged at the knees, no shoes. He also wore a tall, ice-tinkling glass containing some amber fluid, which slopped dangerously as he leaned against the door-frame, waiting for an answer.

'Good afternoon,' I replied. 'My name is Preston. I have an appointment to see Mr Rivers. Three o'clock.'

He nodded carelessly, and took a pull at his drink. I doubted whether it was a health fluid.

'I'm Rivers,' he announced. 'What was it you wanted?'

His tone was arrogant, dismissive. His breath would have felled the average ox. Keeping my voice carefully even, I said.

'The appointment was your idea, Mr Rivers. I was rather hoping you would tell me what it's all about.'

He wasn't the man I'd come to see, and I knew it. I was just stalling to see how far he'd push it. Now he scowled.

'Listen, I'm a very busy man. Can't be expected to remember every little detail. Just remind me who you are.'

It was even money whether I might grab the glass, and see how far I could shove it down his throat. From inside the house, a woman's voice above clacking heels.

'Larry, is that you Larry? Who's that you're talking to?'

He pulled himself negligently upright, and rolled out of view. I turned towards the approaching footsteps. She was in her early thirties, short-cropped black hair brushed to a shine. The face was a tanned oval, with prominent cheekbones and a well-defined nose. Her mouth was very red against the startling teeth. In the shade, I couldn't see the colour of the deep-set eyes that inspected me with cool interest.

'Good afternoon,' I greeted. 'Mr Rivers is expecting me. The name is Preston, Mark Preston.'

She didn't actually say she didn't believe me, but her eyes said it for her.

'Mr — Preston you say? No, I don't think — '

'Three o'clock,' I nodded. I held out my wrist to show I had a watch of my very own.

'It wasn't Larry you wanted, then?'

'No, he was just asking to see could I teach him some manners. We were about to begin when you arrived. Mr Rivers called me on the phone. This morning. Said it was very important. Very confidential.'

She nodded, still uncertain. Then she smiled.

'Forgive me if I seem a little nonplussed. I am Kathryn Nolan, Mr Rivers' confidential secretary. I arrange all his interviews, all his appointments.'

'Not this one, it seems. He spoke to my,' pause, 'confidential secretary himself. She was quite clear on the point.'

I made a mental note that I mustn't let

Florence Digby find out the way I'd described her. That woman already had an inflated enough view of her contribution. Miss Nolan bit her lip. It was a nice lip. I'd have been glad to do it for her.

'Well then, here you are,' she said brightly. 'Perhaps if you would just give me some idea of what this is all about?'

I sighed. The Rivers house seemed to be full of people with nothing to do but check on the owner's affairs.

'Miss Nolan, I don't know. I'm here because he asked me to come. That's the whole story. Full point. Maybe if somebody told him I'm here we could all find out what he wants?'

That seemed to make up her mind.

'Very well, I'll tell him.' She half-turned to go, then looked back at me. 'Oh, please step inside. It's too hot out there.'

I made a half-bow and stepped inside, eyes following the rhythmic swing of slim hips as she disappeared into the gloom. An interesting household so far, I decided. One prospective coiffure model, female, one prospective drunk, male, one confidential secretary who wasn't in the

6

boss's confidence. Female. Very female, I corrected.

The hall told me nothing, except that it was a pleasant place to stand. A curving staircase wound up and away to the sleeping quarters. At the foot stood a pedestal, bearing a bust of some tough-looking character with ruffs at his throat. The kind of guy who smiled at the ladies just before setting fire to their ships a couple of centuries ago. I wondered what he was doing there. It was a cinch his name hadn't been Rivers.

There was a kind of baronial fireplace, with logs ready in position. They'd been in position a long time, to judge by the gleaming copper basket in which they rested. Fires make things dirty, if I recall, and dirty was not a word which sprang to mind about any of the fittings in that house. Above the fireplace, where there ought to have been a portrait of the fourth baron or something, there was a curious rectangular projection, protected by black velvet curtains. About two feet wide, by three deep, it was for all the world like a small cinema screen, standing on its side, and waiting for someone to draw the curtains, so the show could begin.

'Mr Preston?'

I hadn't heard her come back. Turning, I saw her waiting for me, with that provocative half-smile which I would have liked to get accustomed to.

'Please come this way, won't you? Mr Rivers apparently called you while I was busy typing up some reports for him. He forgot to mention it.'

She led me to a pair of ornate white doors, turning a gold handle as she ushered me inside.

'Mr Preston for you.'

The room was long, and high-ceilinged. Books lined two walls, forming a half-frame to the huge empire desk which dominated the far end. Bernard L. Rivers looked at me expectantly. He was younger than I'd realised, no more than mid-forties. His face was strong rather than handsome, a good sweep to the chin and a pronounced aquiline nose. The dark eyes were hooded. Above them a prominent square forehead, and above that a good thatch of thick brown hair. As he rose to greet me, I saw a tall man, six feet three or four inches. The shoulders were powerful beneath the crimson sport shirt. It was cool in the room, but there were beads of perspiration on his brow and his handshake was moist.

'Please sit down, Mr Preston, while we talk.'

The chair was straight-backed, hard leather. Not for sleeping in. A chair to sit on, while we talked. His voice was a disappointment. It ought to be commanding, or resonant, or something like that, emanating from such a big frame. Instead it was meticulous, with the dry sound of snapping twigs.

'Not an auspicious beginning, Mr Preston. It would appear you are ten minutes late.'

He looked at me severely, waiting for an explanation.

'It would appear wrong,' I told him. 'I've been here fifteen minutes trying to get past that pack of busybodies outside.'

Now he leaned back, resting fingertips on the desk, not taking his eyes from me.

'Busybodies?'

'Some kid named Larry, he was first. Then your confidential secretary, who doesn't seem to be in your confidence where I'm concerned.'

'Ah, Larry, yes. My son. My son Laurence, that is. Was he — um — difficult at all?'

'No more difficult than any other young feller who's drinking stuff he can't handle.'

He nodded, digesting this.

'I'm sorry about that. As to Miss Nolan, well, she is a most capable young woman. Quite extraordinarily efficient, and I don't know how I should manage without her. However, this — um — matter I wish to discuss with you is not something to be shouted from the housetops, Mr Preston. In fact, it will not be discussed anywhere except between you and I, in this room. That is to say, if we discuss anything at all.'

My look of surprise was genuine.

'If we discuss anything at all?' I repeated.

'Yes. Please do not get excited. Let me

explain. There is a situation here where, for once in my life, I really cannot manage alone. I do not care for that, Mr Preston. Not at all. However, I do need help. Your kind of help.'

He stopped for a moment to pour out some iced water into a crystal glass. As he raised it to his lips, there was a slight tremor in his hand. Fresh perspiration gleamed dully on his forehead.

'And so,' he continued, 'it is very necessary that I know more about you. Before I tell you things which are personal to me. Painful to me. Have you any objection?'

'Not at all,' I replied. 'But one thing puzzles me. If you haven't already checked me out how did I get here? And if you need some people to refer to — '

He held up a hand to check me.

'I explain myself badly. You are quite right, of course. I have, as you say, checked you out. Most thoroughly. You certainly seem to be the right man for me. But these are other people's judgements, other people's views. Believe me, if this were an ordinary job of work, I would

11

have hired you, sight unseen, on the strength of what I'm told. Now, I wish to add my own assessment.'

It was evident my prospective client was not sending me off to find his missing dog.

'That seems reasonable,' I nodded. 'Fire away, Mr Rivers.'

And he did. He grilled me for twenty exhausting minutes. At the end, he smiled. It was not a warm experience.

'I must say, you seem to justify everything I have been told. And now, the purpose of your visit.

He slid open a drawer, took out some papers and fingered at them thoughtfully. It was as though he was hoping, even now, that something would happen to make it unnecessary to have to tell the story, whatever it was.

'Gold is a beautiful metal,' he said dreamily. 'Do you not agree, Mr Preston?'

'Never had much to do with it,' I confessed. 'It seems to have caused a fair piece of trouble, down the years.'

He ignored that.

'Gold is, or was, my business. Bullion. I

was a dealer for many years. I am a very rich man, as you may have gathered. My personal life has been dogged by tragedy. The legends all say that gold brings no happiness. Romantic nonsense of course. But it is undeniably true that money has brought me no lasting joy. I married very young. In New York. She was a beautiful girl. We had two children, a boy, and later a girl. The boy was Laurence, whom you met outside.'

'There was a girl out there, too,' I told him. 'Pretty kid, seemed to be sunbathing. I didn't get to speak to her.'

'That would be Lynda Lee,' he confirmed. 'Everything went well for us. I was beginning to make my way in the world, had a sound, well-based home life. That was when the first tragedy occurred. The apartment house we lived in caught fire one night. I got my son out, Carol rescued the baby. Then, before I could stop her, she went back inside for her jewellery. She didn't get out the second time. She died in there, for a handful of trinkets. It was a terrible blow.'

It was a good moment to be staring

impassively at the bookshelves. After a moment, he resumed.

'I thought my life was ended, which was a perfectly natural reaction. And of course, I was wrong. There was work to be done, children to rear. So I set myself to it. Rather too hard, my friends used to say. I allowed no time for relaxation, since that side of my life seemed to have closed. Then I saw Judith Harvey in a play on Broadway. You recall the name?'

I racked around the memory banks. No answer.

'I'm sorry,' I confessed, 'I don't really follow the theatre.'

'No.' He seemed to find that an admission of guilt. 'Today, everything is television, I regret to say. But there are a few corners of the world where legitimate theatre survives. Anyway, I saw this play, and I saw Judith. Life began again. A year later, we were married. I was like a young man overnight. My wife was everything any man could ask. Beautiful, charming, witty. And accomplished in the domestic sense, too. That was a considerable surprise, as you may imagine. I decided that it was time to leave the business world, and so I set about winding up my affairs. Not hastily, of course. I allowed myself two years to plan things properly. Then I brought my whole family out here. From now on, it was to be the good life.'

Not bad, I reflected. To be able to cash up in his forties, and live on the fat the rest of his life, Rivers must have been a very big operator. Or a very big thief. It depends on the point of view. To show I was still listening, I said.

'How long ago was this Mr Rivers? I mean, when you moved to Monkton City.'

'Three years. A little over three years. I bought this house, and we all settled in. It all seemed like a dream come true.'

He stared at the papers in front of him. Some were photographs, but I was not close enough to make out any details.

'But something went wrong,' I prompted.

'Very wrong. Tragically wrong. We had a power-boat, the *Messalina Girl*. One of

15

Judith's great joys was to get out into the bay, and drive the boat, full throttle. She was very good, too. A good sailor, perfectly safe. Or so we all thought. Then, two years ago, a little less, she went out one evening, and did not return. She hit something out there, a piece of driftwood or some other debris. As you probably know, those boats are terribly vulnerable at full speed. We shall never know just how it happened. It was one of those nights when the sea-fog appears quite suddenly, like a blanket. It might have been that she was no longer able to see clearly. Anyway, whatever caused the boat to break up, it made a thorough job. Some fisherman found pieces of it.'

'And your wife, Judith?'

'There was no trace of her. Not for days. Then her body was washed up on the shore. I'd been hoping — ' he stopped for a moment, to regain himself ' — hoping it was all a mistake. That perhaps she hadn't been there at all. Perhaps she'd decided to take a few days vacation, and someone else had stolen the boat. That was only one of the straws I clutched at.'

He looked across at me, and there was misery on his face.

'Unless you've experienced something like it, Mr Preston, you will have no idea of the crazy alternatives people will create, in order to avoid accepting an obvious truth.'

'I've seen it before,' I assured him. 'You've certainly had more than a fair share of bad luck. And this was almost two years ago, you say?'

It was my gentle way of suggesting maybe we could speed the story up a little. He was scarcely going to ask me to investigate what happened to the *Messalina Girl*. Now, he nodded, as though he'd taken the point.

'You may feel that I've spent too long sketching in all this background history, but I assure you it's all relevant. Two days ago, this came in the mail.'

'This' was a sheet of white paper, which he passed over the desk. There was a message on it, made up of words cut out from newspapers and pasted in uneven lines. It read:

'Vengeance is mine, saith the Lord, but sometimes he's too long-winded. I won't wait.'

I stared at it for a while, wondering what it meant. The sender had had problems with 'saith'. It was in two halves, the 's' and the 'a' from one word, the 'ith' from another. I shrugged my shoulders, and passed it back.

'Vengeance?' I queried. 'Just some hothead, I imagine. Or does someone have a reason to be avenged? You know, Mr Rivers, I'm going to have to level with you on this. I don't have a cat's chance in hell of tracing the sender.'

He smiled that thin smile again.

'I appreciate that, but you anticipate me. What you say is perfectly true. In fact, that's what the police told me.'

Now I was listening very hard.

'You took that to the police? Well then, I don't quite see — '

'No, I'm sure you do not. But there is more.'

He handed over a second message, not unlike the first in its general appearance. This one said

'Even Ayesha perished finally in the flames.'

Whoever pasted it up had a whale of a time making up the name.

'Ayesha,' I repeated. 'Beats me. I'm afraid my knowledge of the Bible isn't that good, Mr Rivers. What does it mean?'

'It doesn't relate to the Bible,' he corrected. 'It's an old adventure story by a man named H. Rider Haggard. Most people call it She. A story about a beautiful woman thousands of years old, who stays beautiful by standing in a sacred flame. Finally the flame kills her.'

Now I had it.

'Thank you. But what does it mean?'

'It means someone intends to set fire to the house. This house.'

Ayesha. Lynda Lee? Miss Nolan? It seemed unlikely. Seeing my puzzlement, Rivers said:

'It's referring to Judith's portrait. It is very dear to me, and it's also extremely valuable. One of the last paintings Douglas Westley did. That makes it valuable to the rest of world as well. But I'm not concerned with that side of it.'

'Who'd want to burn a painting?' I wondered. 'What sense would it make?'

But already I was suspicious. If the painting was worth a lot of money, it would be insured. Maybe Rivers wasn't as well-fixed as he was letting me think. Anybody can cut up newspapers. To my surprise, he said:

'As to that, I can tell you exactly who.'

And he handed across a glossy photograph of a woman's face. A good-looking blonde, the attraction for me slightly marred by too knowing an expression. It was a publicity still, and the name of the photographer was printed on the back. A New York firm.

'They're making the arsonists better looking these days,' I commented. 'Who is she?'

I held on to the picture. Rivers' face was serious.

'Her name is — or was — Olivia Jayne Hart. She may have changed it. An actress. In fact she was Judith's stand-in for a time, or would have been if a certain motion-picture deal had gone through. The resemblance was quite remarkable in some lights. But Olivia never had the sweetness on her face. Nor inside her. From a distance, you could be confused. Close to, never.'

'I see,' I murmured, not seeing at all. 'And why would this girl want to burn down your house? And the portrait?'

He shook his head.

'Not the house. Not really. It's the portrait she wants destroyed.' There was a pause while he tried looking at me. Then not looking at me. We were getting to the hard part. 'It's all I have left of Judith, you see. Olivia knows what it means to me.'

I picked over the two or three hundred questions I wanted to ask.

'What makes you so certain Miss Hart is involved?'

'Because she phoned. Yesterday. She called to ask whether I was receiving my mail. In other words, those ridiculous threats.'

'I see. And what are the police doing?'

His mouth went very tight as he said, 'I haven't told the police.'

'But I thought you said — '

'About the anonymous threat, yes. The

first one. I would have reported the second one automatically, but once I knew who was responsible I couldn't go to the police.'

'So you came to me,' I finished.

'Just so.'

I stared at Olivia Jayne Hart. She seemed to be looking at something over my shoulder.

'Mr Rivers, I realise this is all very difficult for you, but you're going to have to tell me more. In fact, all of it.'

He mopped at his face with snow-white linen.

'Yes, of course. I understand that. The fact is, you see, Miss Hart and I — that is, until I met Judith — this is all very painful.'

It always is.

'Let me see if I have the picture,' I suggested. 'You and Miss Hart were seeing each other, before you met your second wife. After that, it was goodbye Miss Hart.'

'You make it sound very brutal,' he objected.

'Brutal or no, that's about what

happened, isn't it? In fact, if there was some business relationship between the two women, it was probably Miss Hart who introduced you in the first place. Am I right?'

Rivers nodded.

'Exactly so. Olivia and I were close, quite close. Not in the marrying sense. Not from my side anyway. She was an ambitious girl, she loved the bright lights, the expensive eating places, I could provide all these things, and I did, gladly. That was my end of our — um — arrangement. The question of anything more serious or permanent never entered my head. We both needed someone to relax with. That was the extent of it.'

'You thought,' I amended. 'Then, when you met your future wife, you wanted to sever the relationship. Miss Hart's reaction was not at all what you'd expected.'

Rivers raised his arms in despair.

'Absolutely correct,' he snapped. 'I'll never understand women. We'd been close for a few months. It had all been most enjoyable. Her attitude astonished me. She practically accused me of jilting her. It was a very unpleasant time. In fact, and I'm not proud of this, she became quite ill, and had to go away. I paid the bills, naturally.'

Naturally. I decided I was liking Rivers less and less. Still, if a man only worked for people he liked, a man could get hungry fast.

'Well, now I think I understand what Miss Hart has against you, and why she wouldn't harbour any love for your late wife. That leaves two areas unexplained. First, why has she taken so long to revenge herself, and second, why not call in the police?'

'Ah.'

He was avoiding my eyes again. People who do that worry me. It means either they have something shameful to say, or they're going to tell me lies.

'So far as your first question is concerned, it refers back to her illness. I'm afraid it was really rather severe. I had no way of knowing this when we first met, but there was in fact some family history of mental disorder. Olivia was always a highly-strung young woman. When the

— um — matter of my marriage to Judith arose, it seemed to be the final straw that tipped her over the edge into instability. She became quite out of control, until finally her family had no option but to have her certified. It was terribly sad.'

You must have been all broken up, I thought sourly. Aloud, I asked

'Are you saying that she is now free again? That she's cured?'

'Heavens, no. By no means. No, what has happened is that the poor girl has left the sanatorium. Someone must have relaxed their vigilance for a time. Anyway, she esc — that is, she walked out. And now she's loose, and threatening me. Everyone here, in fact. Fire is not a selective agent, Mr Preston.'

But I still wanted more.

'Let me understand you, Mr Rivers. Are you saying this girl has come clear across the United States, just to find you?'

I tried to keep disbelief from my tone, but maybe I didn't try too hard. Rivers flushed.

'No,' he returned coldly. 'The family found some time ago that they no longer had the resources to meet sanatorium costs. They approached me, and I felt, in all the circumstances, I should assume the responsibility myself. Not that I blame myself for what happened, you must understand. But I had been fond of Olivia. I couldn't see her in an institution.'

Bully for you.

'So, when you moved out here, you had her transferred.' I made it a statement. 'What was the name of the hospital?'

'It isn't a hospital. It is the Franklin Hoskins Residential Unit. A small, discreet place. Dr Hoskins is well known in the field of psychiatric medicine. She has been in good hands. I am told she receives nothing but the finest treatment.'

He was making too much of it, I thought. He didn't have to explain himself to me. Not if he was the all-round good guy he was setting himself up to be. I tapped at the photograph.

'After all this time, she isn't going to look like this any more. I suppose it's too much to hope there's a more recent picture?'

'I'm afraid not. Places — er — establishments of that kind do not have much need for such things.'

'No,' I agreed. 'Well, that explains why it took so long. But what about the police?'

'Absolutely not,' and his tone was final. 'They would treat her as no more than a common criminal. The very best she could hope for in that direction would be commitment to a criminal asylum. I could not begin to contemplate such a thing. There can be no question of it. No police.'

Neither of us spoke for a while, each busy with his thoughts.

'Mr Rivers,' I said finally, 'I don't think I can help you. This is a big city, the girl could be anywhere. Young women get lost every day of the week. The Missing Persons Bureau works around the clock, all year long. Their success rate is not what they would like. What chance do you think one man would have?'

He looked at me disdainfully.

'Naturally, I had thought of these things before I called you. Olivia is not like any other missing person. You don't have to go and find her, Mr Preston. She's coming here, she said so. All we have to do is wait.'

That made sense. But I still raised an objection.

'In that case, you don't really need anyone at all. You could grab her yourself.'

'As to what I might be able to do, and what I intend to do, you must permit me to be the judge. I cannot remain awake twenty four hours a day, nor do I intend to try. And when she comes, what then? She might have acquired a gun of some kind. She's talking of fire. Perhaps she'll bring kerosene. Why, in this day and age, you can even walk into a garden supplies store and buy a flamethrower. I believe I have normal courage, Mr Preston, but I am an ordinary man. Violence is foreign to me. I need a professional.'

That made sense. Just how professional I would feel, facing a madwoman with a flamethrower, was a matter for my private thoughts.

'I see what you mean,' I conceded.

'Especially about staying awake continuously. I can't do that either. There's a man who works for me now and then. A good man. I'm going to need him.'

His face was unhappy.

'This man,' he queried, 'how much would you tell him?'

'Almost nothing at all,' I assured him. 'He'll be a straightforward watchdog, nothing more. And I'll need somewhere to sleep.'

'Sleep?'

Brown eyebrows shot up.

'Mr Rivers, it's past four o'clock. We still have a few hours of daylight. I want to get a clear idea of the layout of this house, locate Sam Thompson — that's the man I mentioned — and get him out here. If the lady is coming, it could easily be tonight. I also want to meet everyone in the house, so that they understand I must have complete freedom to act. Right now, I want to see this portrait, since it seems to be the root of all the trouble.'

'You are acting as though you've been hired, Mr Preston,' he reproved.

I grinned mirthlessly.

'Oh, I'm hired, Mr Rivers. I've been hired from the minute you started telling me the background. You weren't going to reveal all that, and then not hire me. Let's not waste the daylight.'

He nodded, and stood up.

'Yes. I think I may have the right man. And you are right about the time factor. We must get on quickly. Come with me.'

As he began to move around the desk, the phone trilled. We both looked at the intruder. Rivers shrugged, and picked it up. At once, his face changed.

'Olivia?' he said. Then he cupped his hand over the mouthpiece quickly. 'In the hall. Quick. Telephone. Listen in.'

I ran out quickly, saw an extension phone on a small table. Grabbing it up, I pressed it to my ear.

'No wait, please, listen,' came Rivers' anxious voice.

There was a click. Then silence. More clicking, as Rivers agitated the button at his end, calling 'Livvy, Livvy'. Then nothing.

It's odd how small things give people

away. That intimate 'Livvy' and the pleading, anxious tone of his voice told me a lot about the relationship between my new employer and Olivia Jayne Hart.

I was still holding the dead receiver when he appeared at the open doorway. His cheeks were twitching, and the sweat was back.

'Did you hear all that?' he demanded.

I shook my head.

'I didn't hear any of it,' I admitted, replacing the receiver.

'She said, 'why don't we stay home tonight, and have a nice fire'. I tried to talk with her, but she just laughed and hung up.'

His face was sick with worry. I said

'It's all of a pattern, Mr Rivers. The person doing the threatening is just as agitated as the people being threatened. They have to keep in touch, to refuel their own determination. Try not to worry about it. After all, you're no worse off than before. You've just been reminded.'

'Yes, yes of course. It's just that — well,

never mind. You're quite right. There's no
point in sitting around wringing my
hands. The thing to do is get on with the
precautions. Please come with me.'

He led me back into the entrance hall,
motioning me to a spot by the door. Then
he took a flat black box from his pocket. I
looked at it with interest.

'Control panel,' he explained. 'One of
my main hobbies. Electronics. Look over
the fireplace.'

He was directing my eyes to the odd
structure I'd noticed when I first arrived.
The thing that looked like an up-ended
movie screen. His fingers moved on the
panel. Above my head, and behind me
there was a whirring sound. I craned
around, to see a second pair of curtains
moving smoothly aside. They were
directly opposite the fireplace, and as
they opened, the brilliant afternoon
sunshine struck through, for all the world
like the beam from a projector, lighting
up the facing curtains.

Rivers pressed more buttons. The
curtains on the main structure now began
to move. It was all very theatrical, but just

the same, I felt an excitement rising inside me, as I waited for my first glimpse of the lady who'd been the cause of all the trouble.

The beautiful Judith Harvey Rivers.

2

The curtains were deceiving. All they revealed was a further covering, of curving steel shutters. These in turn began to move apart, sliding effortlessly back into a recess.

Then I saw her.

The face was a near-perfect oval, nose firm above a wide, smiling mouth. Her chin was determined without being aggressive, and the smile carried over into confident, deep-blue eyes. My fingers itched to touch the rich, milky velvet of her skin. Small, snug ears disappeared into a tumbling and dancing cascade of golden hair. The whole set of her head conveyed a superb serenity, an aura of tranquil self-knowledge, as a being apart.

I've seen a thousand beautiful women, expensive women, but this one was more. This one was the ultimate, the standard by which other women could measure themselves.

I simply stood there, staring.

'Well Mr Preston?'

The voice was an intrusion, an invasion of privacy.

Nettled, I shifted my reluctant eyes away from the portrait. Rivers stood, watching my face. His smile was half-sad, reminding me that we were looking at his dead wife.

'Oh, excuse me,' I muttered, shame-faced.

'Most understandable,' he assured me. 'She always had that effect on people. Westley really captured the essence of her. He wasn't one to flatter his subjects, as you may know.'

I tried to look knowledgeable. Luckily, he didn't want to pursue it. Instead, he went on.

'And what do you think of the frame?'

Outside of being vaguely aware that the picture had to come to an end some-where, I hadn't even noticed the frame. Now I looked. The portrait was edged by heavy, ornate, gold-coloured wood. Four inches wide all around, and at least a full inch thick. The workmanship of the decoration seemed to be of a very high order, the kind of thing I always associate in my mind with old European paintings in cathedrals and museums.

'It looks very impressive,' I granted. 'I imagine it isn't too easy these days to find a craftsman who knows how to produce that kind of work.'

Rivers nodded. There was a faint gleam in his eyes, almost as if he was kind of joking at my expense. I didn't mind. Carving was out of my line, and that was no secret.

'And the material,' he pressed, 'what would you think it is?'

I thought for a moment.

'Well, I know they use hard wood, because anything else gets attacked by bugs. That's as far as I go. Maybe teak, oak, I really wouldn't know, Mr Rivers. Suppose you tell me.'

He stroked gently at his chin with a middle finger.

'What would you say if I told you it was gold?'

'You mean the decoration on the top? I'd say it was beautiful workmanship. It would also be expensive.'

'It would,' he agreed. 'But I'm not speaking of the surface decoration. I mean the whole thing. Gold, Mr Preston. Solid gold.'

Now I looked at it really hard. 'Solid gold,' I repeated dully. Then I had an objection. 'But the weight? I wouldn't know the figures, but the weight would be colossal. A thing that size would never just hang on a wall.'

'You are absolutely correct,' he agreed. 'The structure of the wall had to be reinforced to support the weight. The picture had to be winched into position and then secured. It doesn't hang there at all. It is part of the wall. That's why I do not concern myself too much about thieves. It would take four men with special equipment a whole day to remove it.'

Now I understood the steel shutters. The curtains were obvious. They were to prevent the strong sunshine from fading the colours. The shutters were security. I shook my head in amazement.

'Solid gold. What must it be worth?'

'It's worth, to me, is the value of its contribution to the portrait. It is a setting, the only suitable setting, and no more. And now, I'm afraid we must cover it again.'

I stared hard at Judith Harvey Rivers, not wanting to miss a moment of her, until the steel shutters clicked firmly together. Then I pulled my thoughts back to the present.

'With all that protection, nobody can get at the picture to damage it. It can't be carried away. So the only way to attack is by fire. Am I getting it right?'

'Absolutely.'

I glanced around the hall, looking at it now from an entirely new angle.

'Wood. Everything is wood. The place would certainly burn.' Looking up at the ceiling, I asked 'is that a sprinkler system I see up there?'

'Yes it is. And most efficient, I'm assured. But only against a normal fire. A blaze which started deliberately, with chemical agents of some kind, would be too much for it.'

And even if the system finally beat the

flames, I reflected, the heat alone would do untold damage to the portrait.

'I'm no pyrotechnics man, but I'm sure what you say makes sense. Your concern is becoming more understandable by the minute. Could I see the rest of the house? No need to go into anybody's room. Just so I have the layout.'

'We'll begin upstairs.'

It didn't take long. I stared out from an upper window across the hills. Here and there, a group of buildings would stand out, but they were all very far away. Too far to hope people would come a-running with water buckets. The view from the rear was much the same, except for a sudden shining glint, a mile or so away.

'That would be the reservoir?' I queried.

'Yes. A little too far to be much help here, I'm afraid. An interesting spot, if you're ever that way. Our local wild-life tends to gather there for the water.'

We were now overlooking the back of the house. A large circular swimming pool looked blue and inviting as it sparkled under the sunlight. There were a few white tables and chairs, with coloured umbrellas dotted around. The girl I now knew to be Lynda Lee was sprawled casually on the grass, flicking idly at a coloured magazine. There was no sign of the boy or Kathryn Nolan.

Back downstairs, I took a quick peek at the living room, dining room, kitchen, and a small study where we found Miss Nolan busy typing.

'Hello again,' she greeted.

'Kathryn, Mr Preston will be with us for the next few days,' my escort told her. 'Tell Pedro and Anna to include him in meal arrangements, please.'

'Certainly, Mr Rivers.'

The dark eyes were wide with curiosity, but she asked no questions. Not then. I knew they'd be coming.

We ended up back in the gold merchant's study.

'Have you seen all you want to see?' he asked.

'Thank you, yes. I have a good general idea of the house. Tell me about the outside lighting.'

It wasn't very impressive. A few

ornamental lights, all close to the house. As I listened, I wondered what else I'd been expecting. Not too many private homes go in for floodlights in case of approaching arsonists.

'Bear with me if this sounds crazy,' I begged, 'but does Miss Hart have a pilot's licence?'

'A pilot's — ? No, no I don't think so. Not as far as I am aware, at least. Why do you ask?'

'Helicopter,' I told him. 'The ideal way to attack this house would be to use a chopper. She could sit up there and do just what she wanted, and there'd be no way of stopping her. But it's a pretty wild thought. I'm just covering angles.'

He nodded, thinking about it.

'As you say, a wild thought. But it's the kind of distorted thinking we'll have to do. We're dealing with a distorted mind. There's a charter company over at Monkton Field, isn't there? It might be an idea just to check with them.'

'There are two. And yes, I think so. I know the security people over there. I'll have them notify us of all the private hire

41

jobs for the next couple of days. They'll make a charge of course.'

He waved a hand.

'Don't worry about it. Money, fortunately, is no problem. What will you do now?'

'I'll have to get back into town, make some arrangements. One or two things could be starting right away, if I could use a telephone.'

'Of course, of course. You'll probably need to use one quite often while you're here. Don't think me rude, but I would like to carry on with some work, now that I know the problem is in your hands. So would you mind using the phone in the living room? Then I could be getting on.'

I promised to be back by nightfall, and went off to make my calls. The phone stood on a small table by open French doors. It was cool in the room, the glaring sunlight cutting off in a straight line of shade thrown by the roofed verandah.

'Preston Investigations. Good afternoon.'

Florence Digby sounded cool and efficient, as always. Gives the clients a good impression. I asked her to round up Sam Thompson, and have him at my office in twenty minutes. Also to tell him he could be away from home for two days. That wouldn't cause any big disturbance. Home, for Sam, was just a room, any room, where he could catch up on his sleep.

'And I want you to contact a photographic agency in New York. It's called, wait a minute — ' I looked on the back of Olivia Jayne Hart's picture — 'Nathan's Artistry. A Plaza number. You have a pencil?'

She always has a pencil. I told her about Olivia Hart's publicity still. What I wanted was any record they had of the transaction. Home address, anything at all.

'One last thing. There is a Dr Franklin Hoskins who runs a private sanatorium somewhere in the area. Find out where it is, and check him out with the Medical Register. By the time you've done all this, I ought to be back in the office.'

'Very well.'

I put down the phone, and lit an Old

Favourite. Smoke curled away from me and out through the open doors. It was very peaceful there, I decided. A spot where a man could have a quiet smoke and think about things. To be more direct, to think about the haunting face of Judith Harvey Rivers.

'Oh, it's you.'

A shadow fell across the flagged terrace. Larry Rivers stood looking in at me. He seemed unfamiliar without the glass. I didn't need any more of his kind of conversation, and made no reply.

'You gonna take the job?' he demanded.

I stared at his handsome face, marred by the sour twist of his mouth.

'Job?' I stalled.

'Sure, the job. My illustrious and respected parent offered you a job, didn't he?'

'What makes you think so?'

He swaggered inside, and dropped heavily into a chair, one leg dangling over the arm. His bare feet were dirty.

'It's a cinch you're no salesman. My old man wouldn't let one past the front porch. What kind of job is it?'

Despite the casual sprawl, and the bored expression, I realised he really wanted to know. Why would it be important, I wondered?

'If you want to know why I'm here, I suggest you ask your father,' I told him carefully.

'Huh. Hey, could I have one of those?'

He jabbed a forefinger towards my cigarette. I shrugged, took out the pack and passed it to him. He produced kitchen matches.

'Old Favourites, huh? Kind of expensive, aren't they?'

'I'm kind of an expensive feller,' I replied.

He laughed. A short, snorting sound.

'I'll bet. The old man never buys anything but the best. And he does buy everything. Especially people. What's he buying you for?'

There was no point in quarrelling with the boy, if I was going to be around the house for the next few days.

'My name is Preston,' I said. 'I'm a kind of security expert. Your father wants me to help out with something he's working on. You're Larry, aren't you?'

'You got it. Scion of a noble house. You think this is a noble house. I could tell you different. Security huh? What's he buying this time. Fort Knox?'

'He's thinking about it,' I replied. 'First off, he wants me to check it's real gold in there. Doesn't want to get stuck with a pile of plastic bricks.'

He looked at me narrowly, then gradually the sullen expression went away from his mouth, to be replaced by the ghost of a grin. It made a pleasant change.

'Jokes, yet. You're some strange kind of security man. I always understood they were hard guys. No sense of humour, and not much imagination.'

'Just the cheap ones,' I assured him. 'Your father buys nothing but the best.'

I'd spoiled it. At the mention of his father, the boy's face went grim again. He looked away from me. I got up and walked out on the terrace. The girl had abandoned the magazine, and seemed to have fallen asleep. I stared across open country. From this level, the hills seemed bigger than from the upper floor. There was no sign of the reservoir, but a distant flight of birds wheeled and cavorted above the spot where I knew it had to be. I finished the cigarette and went back in the house. Larry had disappeared again. Maybe he'd decided to wash those feet.

Rivers looked up from his desk when I tapped on his door.

'Did you make your calls?'

'Yes. I have to get back into town now. By the way, I've just been talking with your son again.'

His face was expressionless.

'Was he still drinking?'

'Not this time. But he did make me remember something. If I'm going to be around here, it can hardly be a secret from the family. I need a cover story. I already told him I'm some kind of security man.'

'You're quite right,' he nodded. 'You have to be explained. Let us think of something.'

'Mr Rivers,' I began, 'we've talked about the woman, and the picture, and

47

the house. So far, you haven't said anything about the danger to the rest of the family. Don't you think they ought to have some kind of warning?'

'Danger? What danger? Olivia wouldn't harm them. It's me she'll be after, if anyone. I even doubt that, you know. No, it's Judith's portrait. That is the objective.'

I couldn't make up my mind whether he really believed it, or just wasn't thinking straight. Now I shook my head.

'It won't do,' I said decisively. 'It won't do at all. Maybe you've never seen a fire, except on the news. I've been close up, more than once. Fire is fast, Mr Rivers, faster than people can imagine unless they've been involved. It doesn't start in one corner of the room and burn steadily across. One minute there's nothing, the next everything goes. It's possible to be standing just a few yards away from people who are being burned to death, and not be able to do a damned thing to help them. I'm not being dramatic, I've stood there. It's not an experience a man forgets. Objectives? Try telling a twenty-foot sheet of flame what it's objective is.'

At least he listened.

'Do you know, I'm glad you're here. And you are, of course, quite correct. I've been thinking in the most selfish terms, and I thank you for pointing it out. This is such a personal matter, so really private between Olivia and me. It never entered my head that there could be real danger for my family. That wouldn't be her intention, I'm sure of that. But you make your point. You make it well. It wouldn't matter what she intended. They have to be told something. Something that will put them on the alert, without frightening them too much. What do you suggest?'

I was relieved that he wasn't going to be stubborn.

'Kidnap?' I offered. 'You're a wealthy man. It might be worth a try, putting the snatch on you.'

'H'm.'

He thought about it.

'But how would I know about it? I don't imagine such people send out word in advance. Surprise has to be everything.'

That was too accurate to argue against. I tried again.

'Maybe it was general threat? Not naming you by name, but just applying to all big dealers in gold.'

Rivers looked doubtful.

'A bit far-fetched, isn't it. But you give me an idea. I am, or was, a member of an international bullion cartel. It involved people in Rome, Paris, London, all over. One or two of the more militant pressure groups have made nasty noises in the past.'

He stared across for comment. I nodded.

'Then that's it. We bring the nasty noises up to date. These people intend to strike somewhere in the world. Nobody can say where, or who will be the victim. So you've all agreed it would be sensible to take precautions. How does it sound?'

'Well, it isn't the most convincing story I ever heard. But, very well.'

I left him, and went back out into the sunshine. In the doorway, I paused to take a look at the black curtains above the fireplace, willing my memory to see through them to the hidden painting. Shaking my head at my own foolishness, I went past the soothing fish pond and down to the car.

'Hey.'

With the door half-open, I looked back. Larry Rivers stood at the top of the steps, looking down.

'How's for a lift into town? My car's being fixed, and I could bring it back here.'

I didn't want him along, but there was no reason I could think up for refusing.

'Sure.'

He ambled down towards me, making me wait. Scion of a noble house, wasn't that what he's said? Some scion.

When he finally got in beside me, he sprawled out resting his head on the back of the seat. Neither of us spoke on the trip. His eyes were closed, but I knew he wasn't asleep. When we hit the city limits, he opened one eye and screwed his head towards me.

'You wanna lend me twenty bucks?' he demanded.

'Why?'

'Like to pick up a coupla things while I'm in town,' he replied.

I looked at him, detecting a note almost of pleading in the voice, and wondering about it.

'I didn't mean what do you want the money for,' I told him. 'I meant why ask me? The banks are open.'

That brought a short, rasping laugh.

'Oh brother,' he sighed. 'Get you. Listen, the only way I'm going to get money out of any bank is with a sub-machine gun. My dear old white-haired daddy has seen to that.'

No more pleading now, just sourness. Like the last time he'd spoken of his father. Well if his old man kept him short of money, there'd have to be reasons.

'I guess not, Larry. You'd better take it up with him.'

He snorted, but I could sense he'd been expecting the answer.

'You two oughta get married,' he snapped. 'You'd make a lovely couple. Drop me here.'

'Here' was an intersection well clear of the city centre. There wasn't any car repair service within blocks. Still, that was his problem. I pulled over to the kerb, and let him out.

'See you back at the house.'

He made no reply, sticking his thumbs into torn pockets, and shuffling away. Looking the way he did, it would be no surprise to learn he'd been vagged by the first police officer who spotted him.

I headed for the office.

3

When I opened the outer door, Florence Digby was in earnest conversation with a large shambling man, whose whole appearance shrieked of neglect.

'Afternoon, Miss Digby. Come inside, Sam.'

Sam Thompson has a problem. Possessed of the most monumental thirst in town, he has to match it against a no-income situation. Any bartender will explain to you the background and history of this problem, which is not unique to Thompson, nor even to my home town. But the solution is the same, any town you care to mention. No money, no booze. And so, far more often than he would elect to do it, Sam finds himself having to do some kind of work, this being the most acceptable method of latching onto the bread demanded by those unfeeling bartenders. The work he does best is my kind.

Leg-work, surveillance, sniffing out scraps of information. Stuff like that. If he'd only stick to it, he'd have his own office, his own Digby in no time at all.

'Sit down, Sam. We have a lot to do, and not much time.'

He settled heavily opposite me, and waited.

'The client is a man named Rivers. He owns this valuable painting. Somebody wants to destroy it. We have to stop them. It'll mean spending a night or two out at the house. You'd better pick up a couple of bedrolls for a start.'

His face wrinkled up.

'Oh no,' he protested. 'Not the wide open spaces scene? Listen, I'm just a city boy. That cowboy stuff gives me rheumatism.'

'It will also give you enough dough to buy your own still,' I countered. 'So just listen. There's a doctor, name of Hoskins, Franklyn Hoskins. Florence should have some preliminary information on him when you leave. Find out about him, what kind of place he runs. And get yourself cleaned up, Sam. You oughta be ashamed.'

We both grinned.

'Oh, I am,' he assured me. 'All the time. How can a man keep his self-respect, when he hires out as a casual ranch-hand? When do we start?'

'We already started. Here's the address.' I scribbled on a piece of paper. 'I'll bet you don't have a car, right?'

'You just won a bet,' he nodded.

'O.K. Rent one. They can refer to Miss Digby for clearance. Be out at the house some time after nine. By ten, certain.'

He got up.

'Is this going to be heavy work? Because, if it is, I have a friend sort of keeping an eye on some equipment.'

What he meant was, his gun was in hock. Again.

'How much is it in for?'

'Twenty.'

I raised my eyebrows in surprise.

'You let him keep that thing for twenty dollars? Why, it must be worth — '

'I know what it's worth,' he interrupted, 'but I always take out the hammer. Without that, all the man has is junk metal. It's kind of a precaution of mine. In case the guy has a lapse of memory, and sells my piece to somebody else.'

I put two tens on the table. Reluctantly. One rule I have, about guys like Sam Thompson. Never let them close to ready cash.

'Sam?'

He rolled the tired face from side to side.

'Don't worry, Preston. I'm not going to louse up a chance to buy my own still.'

'All right. I'll catch you later, at the house.'

After he'd gone, I opened a drawer and took out the small notebook in which I list telephone numbers. The man I wanted had a Boulevard number. As I dialled, I was recalling the last time Josh Holland and I had a conversation. It had been three o'clock in the morning, after a long night of chasing our tails around various parts of the Strip. We'd been trying to catch up with a guy who wanted to return a piece of pottery that had been mislaid. With me, a jug is a jug. It holds liquids, and you pour from it. But it seems if you have a very old jug, one that's been around since the Greeks, then you don't just have a jug. What you have is a piece of pottery, a rarity, and something which is worth a lot of money. Strange thing when you think about it. Mostly, stuff which is secondhand is a real drag on the market. But if it's so secondhand no one can even recall the original owner, it gets to be valuable. Anyway, this jug had been stolen from a private collection, and the owner wanted it back. He wasn't concerned about the money, nor even very interested in catching the thief. There was a space in one of his display cabinets, and he wanted it refilled. That was all he cared. I was involved, because that's my job. Holland came along because he'd know if the jug being offered was the real stuff. We finally tracked down this thief in some rattrap off Vine. It turned out the guy was no ordinary mug, but knew his art-world, and he and Holland hit it off straight away. They sat around, yakking it up, while I sat around, holding the jug. When

I finally managed to part them, they were like big buddies. I hadn't seen him since.

'This is the New Holland gallery. May I help you?'

A woman's voice, smooth like cream. I really ought to keep up more with Holland.

'Is Mr Holland around?' I queried. 'I'm a friend of his. Mark Preston.'

'Just a moment Mr Preston. I'll see if he's available.'

Nice, I reflected. Not 'hang on'. Not 'wait a minute'. Instead, 'I'll see if he's available'. That's the kind of talk you get when you pay the kind of money it costs to go shopping at the New Holland Gallery. Then his voice came on.

'This is Joshua Holland speaking. Mr Preston, did you say?'

'I did,' I confirmed. 'I'm in the stolen jug business, remember? The Monty collection. We had a busy time tracking one of his pieces.'

The voice warmed up.

'Oh, that Preston. That was an exciting piece of business, wasn't it? Yes, of course, how are you?'

I said I was fine, and how was he, and he was fine, and then I got to the point.

'I'm sure you can help me again if you will. No jugs. This time it's paintings. Does the name Douglas Westley mean anything?'

There was a pause.

'Yes it does. I don't think we should be talking on the telephone. Could we meet somewhere?'

I thought it was odd.

'Well, I don't have a lot of time — ' I demurred.

'There's a place close to here. Just a plain bar, called Mike's. Do you know it?'

I knew it, and said I'd be there in fifteen minutes. After I put down the phone, I buzzed for Florence. She came in, cool as ever, carrying the inevitable pad.

'Thompson gone?' I asked.

'Yes. I told him what I'd learned about Dr Hoskins. Not very much, I'm afraid. He's just a highly qualified man, who runs a very expensive establishment, and is extremely well regarded.'

I nodded. Florence had evidently been

hoping for a back-street abortionist, with a string of convictions.

'Fine. Did you raise New York?'

'Yes, I did. Not very helpful, I'm afraid. I had a good talk with that number. It now belongs to a construction company. The woman I spoke with knew all about the photographic people, Nathan's Artistry. They were very prominent in the theatre, and the advertising world. But the business relied heavily on the personality of Mr Nathan himself. When he died, the firm quickly collapsed. She wasn't able to help with any records, nor even with anyone else I could ask.'

'H'm.'

It wasn't important, not really. Just that it would have been helpful to round out the story on Olivia Jayne Hart.

'Open a file, Miss Digby. Client's name is Rivers.'

I told her what little I knew, leaving out some of the drama. For all her cool professionalism, Florence worries too much. If she got a mental picture of Thompson and me swapping arguments with a flamethrower she wouldn't get any sleep.

'So you may be away from the office for a few days?'

'I hope not,' I denied. 'No point in us both sitting out there when it's daylight. I'll try to look in some time tomorrow.'

'And if I could have the number of the Rivers house please.'

Once we had everything all written up, she closed the book.

'Is that it?' she asked.

'That's it.'

'Thank you. I didn't mention it before, because I didn't want to disturb your train of thought on this new case, but there was a strange telephone call a little over an hour ago.'

'How, strange?'

'A man called. Said he was looking for a Mr Preston, but he wasn't sure if he had the right man. He only met his Preston once, and hadn't taken his telephone number.'

'What did he want?'

'We didn't get that far. He asked me to describe you physically.'

'And after you told him I was tall, Wasp and handsome?'

She sniffed.

'Those were not exactly the terms I used' — I'll bet, I thought — 'and after I'd told him, he said no, he must have the wrong man. His Preston was a lot shorter, a swarthy complexion.'

I didn't care for that. It isn't good for the image to have too many of these short swarthy Prestons infesting the streets.

'Well that was the end of it, huh?'

She coloured slightly.

'Not entirely. He said well, never mind, and what was I doing tonight, and every night. I decided the man was drunk.'

I grinned.

'You should of taken him up. You might have located this other Preston, and I could of bribed him to change his name. Never mind, don't take it too much to heart. And thanks for telling me.'

I went out to find Mike's.

★   ★   ★

63

Where I come from, the buildings are joined together, both sides of the street, every street. If a gap appears, more than six feet across, there's a guy who rushes in with half-a-dozen stools and a few bottles. Then he closes the gap with a sheet of boarding containing one narrow door. He buys his cousin a white apron and puts him in charge of the bottles. Then he paints his cousin's name on the door. Steve, Butch, Eddie, or whatever. Suddenly we have a bar. The guy rushes on to the next gap because he has an awful lot of cousins. This one is called Mike.

It was no narrower, no friendlier, no cooler than its hundreds of relatives. Josh Holland sat at the far end of the counter, wiping suds off his nose. I got on to the next stool, and we shook hands.

'What'll you have?'

'Beer.'

Even if I couldn't drink the stuff, I'd get a clean nose.

'What's the mystery, Josh?'

'Mystery?'

'Yeah. You wouldn't talk on the telephone. What gives?'

He stared around at the near-empty bar. Mike stood at the end near the door, picking out losers from a newspaper.

'You mentioned a certain name. We needn't repeat it here. But believe me, if you're on the track of something by that man, we are into some very important business. Those paintings are few and far between. And very expensive. Oh, very.'

'Ah.'

Now I could understand. Holland had jumped to the wrong conclusion. It was natural enough. Why would somebody in my line develop a sudden interest in a painter, unless something unusual had happened? And it was important to know that Westley's work was valuable.

'Little misunderstanding here Josh,' I explained. 'Nobody swiped any painting. This is just personal. What happened was, I've seen one of his portraits, and I can't get it out of my head. I realise there's no way I could buy it, but I wondered if there's a chance of getting a copy. You know, the way you can buy imitation Rembrandts and the rest?'

Holland winced.

'Yes, I do know. Only too well. Some of them you can get if you buy enough breakfast cereal. Ah well, it's a start. At least you're interested enough to ask. That's the way some people get started, you know. In a year or two, we'll be seeing you around the salerooms. Now let's think. Westley copies. He didn't have a big output, just a dozen or so portraits.'

'They're all portraits?'

'Yes. Once he settled down. In the early days, it was landscapes, country scenes. That kind of thing. And watercolours. Pretty bad, most of it. But once he found his strength, there was no holding him. Quite remarkable work. Which one did you see?'

'A woman. Just the head and shoulders. Her name was Judith Harvey Rivers.'

He'd been about to dip his nose into the soap again. Now, the glass mug hit the bartop in his agitation. Mike looked up from his paper at the sudden sound, decided there wasn't going to be any trouble, and bent his head again.

Holland spoke, trying to keep disbelief from his tone.

'You've seen the Rivers portrait?'

'Yes. Just this afternoon. What's so special?'

He looked at me very seriously.

'What's so special is this. I wouldn't be quoted as to the exact number, but at the last count I was given, there aren't twenty people in the world who've ever been allowed to see the Rivers painting. It was his last one, did you know that? How did you manage it?'

I shrugged my shoulders, digesting this new information.

'I wasn't aware I was managing anything. Bernard Rivers asked me out to his house. Matter of business. While I was there, he showed me the picture. It haunts me. I want a copy.'

He shook his head in wonderment.

'Amazing. Forgive me, but I can't get over it. Look, there's a man you have to see. His name is Nigel Bravington. Is it known to you?'

'No, I don't think so. Who is he? And why do I have to see him?'

'He is, or was, Douglas Westley's last pupil. Certainly he knows more about the man and his work than another living soul. He'll be most anxious to talk to you.'

I looked at my watch.

'I don't know, Josh. I have a pretty tight schedule.'

'A few minutes,' he begged. 'It isn't far. And — ' he threw in a carrot — 'if there should be any chance of a copy, Nigel will be the man to tell you.'

That sold me.

'O.K. But I'm not kidding about the time. I really do have to be getting on.'

'Then let's move out.'

4

I might have known the place would be called the Tattered Canvas. You don't expect guys with names like Nigel Bravington to hang around joints called Mike's or Butch's. Hold it on the Butch's though, I thought, looking around at the clientele. The Tattered Canvas was no bar, although you could drink if you wanted. It was a club, occupying two floors above a beauty parlour. There was no natural light anywhere. Walls and windows alike were covered entirely by great swathes of shiny curtain material in what to me were colours that clashed. Orange, black, purple, green, you name it. Concealed lighting suffused from behind the drapes, located in such a way as would ensure not much illumination got through. It would probably be in bad taste if the members were able to see who they were talking with. Here and there, a floor to ceiling column of what had to be oil allowed more light to ascend through different coloured levels, disappearing at the top only to start again at the foot.

Odd-shaped chairs, some black, some plum, and covered in leather were dotted around here and there. I looked around in amazement. Over my shoulder Josh Holland chuckled.

'You get used to it after the first hundred times.'

'No thanks. This memory will last a lifetime. Who are all these characters?'

I waved a hand around at the scattering of people who jabbered and twittered at each other like a pigeons' convention. Some were men and some were women. I imagined. A casual visitor would be unwise to commit himself on that one.

Holland kept his voice low.

'These are the scene people of the art world. And when I say scene, I'm using the ancient Hollywood term. In a scene you would have two or three actors, O.K.? All around would be a lot of people. They might be gladiators, peasants, a lynch mob, it wouldn't matter. All they were doing was blocking in the scene for authenticity. The people who mattered were the actors.'

'You lost me,' I admitted.

'This place is like that,' he developed. 'These are the onlookers, the hopefuls, the would-bes. Pottery, sculpture, architecture, painting, you name it. They like to think they're the in-crowd, but they never make centre-stage. That's for the actors, or in this case the artists. The people who are too busy working their tails off creating things to spend a lot of time on bird-talk. But they have to take an hour off now and then. This is a place to come, to refresh the weary inspiration. Pick up a little admiration and a free drink or two, then back to the chunk of marble or whatever.'

I could see what he meant. Although the chatter was incessant, nobody was really paying any attention to anybody else. There was a good deal of head-tossing and bead-jangling, a lot of quick, darting looks around the place to ensure nothing important was being overlooked. I came in for a good share of these fleeting inspections, but nobody took very long to decide it was safe to overlook me.

'Where does our man fit in all this?' I queried.

'Nigel? He's a new kind of painter. Not in style, but I mean in his approach. Three pictures a year, all commissioned, and that's all the work he needs to do. Mr Bravington has no room for starving in an attic, nor for working himself to death. Once he's guaranteed his income for the year, he devotes the rest of his time to running this place.'

'He's the owner?'

'The owner, the chairman, the bouncer, the whole bit. He even lives here, some of the time. Has a couple of rooms upstairs.'

An artist part of the time, businessman the rest. He'd probably be wearing a smock over a plain grey suit.

'Josh love, you've been holding out. Where did you get your delicious friend?'

The new voice belonged to a small person, not much over five feet tall, immaculate in a suit of green suede. The fair hair was swept up and pinned in a Grecian style, above a carefully made-up face which could be anywhere between thirty and fifty years old.

'Oh hi, Phil. This is a friend of mine, Mark Preston.'

'Divine,' squeaked Phil.

Phyllis? Philip? Who could tell? I half-grinned. Nervously.

'Just too manly. It's the only word, really. Gorgeous. And what's your contribution to this wicked, wicked world, Mark Preston?'

I looked squarely into the mauve-circled eyes.

'I'm a mortuary attendant,' I said seriously.

Phil twittered nervously.

'Marvellous. Too grotesque. Well,' and I got a tap on the arm, 'you've come to the right place, lover. Quite a few of these are overdue for the slab.'

My grin was spontaneous. You couldn't help liking the — what?

'We're looking for Nigel. Is he around?' queried Josh.

'When is he not. I think he's in the Pink Room, talking with some of those terrible students.'

'Fine. Catch you later, Phil.'

As we walked away, Phil said 'Careful how you catch me. I'm rather fragile.'

'Are they all like that?' I questioned.

'Worse, mostly. Phil is one of the sane ones.'

And even then I didn't find out my new friend's sex. Holland led me through a curtained opening into another room. Pink was right. Everything was draped pink, painted pink, stained pink. It was like crashing into a woman's bedroom. At one side of the room, a bunch of youngsters in ragged shirts and jeans stood around. They were so normal, they looked out of place. They were paying a lot of attention to a tall, skinny guy with huge horn-rim glasses on a twenty-five year old nose. He wore a lumberjack shirt and faded khaki pants, and had to be Bravington.

Holland waved an arm at him. The big glasses turned in our direction, and he waved back.

'Help yourself to a drink Josh. Be right with you.'

The voice was pleasant. A calm, certain

sound. Very reassuring, after all the twitter. Josh went behind a small counter.

'You heard what the man said. What's it going to be?'

'Do we dare have anything else but a Pink Lady?'

He shrugged.

'You're drinking it. Personally, I'll stick to beer.'

'Right.'

We'd just taken our first swallow when the fair man broke away from his admiring squad and came over. He looked at me with interest. Holland named names, and we shook hands.

'Preston,' he repeated. 'I'm sure I've heard of you someplace.'

I wasn't going to fill any spaces. Holland jumped in.

'I wanted you two to meet,' he said briskly. 'Mark here is interested in Douglas Westley.'

Now I got a more intense inspection.

'Douglas? Really?'

'Yes, I saw one of his paintings, and I want to know if it's possible to get a print for myself. Some kind of reproduction, you know?'

He wagged his head up and down.

'Not impossible. A few have been produced. Which particular one did you have in mind?'

'Judith Harvey Rivers.'

The effect was instant. Bravington went white, and turned to Holland.

'Get him out of here,' he said tightly. 'How dare you do this to me?'

Josh Holland was at once placatory.

'Hold on, Nigel. You don't understand. He's seen the picture.'

The expression left Bravington's face as quickly as it had come.

'Seen it? Am I hearing correctly? You've seen it?'

I nodded, wondering what he was so excited about.

'This afternoon,' I confirmed. 'I was out at the Rivers house, and her husband showed it to me.'

He passed a hand over his forehead, as if to brush away the furrows which had suddenly been planted there.

'Showed it to you?' he repeated. 'Why?'

It was an odd reaction. So unexpected that I almost told him. Stopping myself in time, I countered 'Why shouldn't he? It's his property.'

'Yes, but — '

He didn't finish the sentence. Instead, he stood quite still, looking at the floor. I'd have given a lot to know what was going through his mind. Then he spoke again.

'Forgive me, for reacting the way I did. There's no way you could know — things. As to your reproduction, I'm sorry. There aren't any of that particular portrait. You ought to take a look at the rest of Douglas's work. Well worthy of study, believe me. If you'd like copies of anything else, I'll certainly do all I can. Be my pleasure.'

He was evidently anxious to compensate for his outburst. Or anxious to get away from the subject of Judith Harvey Rivers. The options were open.

'Could well be,' I agreed. 'But the impact of what I saw this afternoon is still with me. Frankly, I don't think my mind is open enough at the moment to consider alternatives.'

An odd, almost shy grin appeared.

'You certainly were impressed, weren't you? Well, you'll have to take my word that I can understand the way you feel. It is one hell of a picture.'

Not the description I would have chosen, but this was not the moment to challenge it.

'From the way you speak,' I suggested, 'you've seen the portrait yourself.'

He stared at something in the middle distance. When he spoke, the voice sounded oddly distant.

'Oh yes. Yes, I've seen it.'

Then Holland butted in.

'In fact, this is quite an occasion. It isn't every day a man can find two people in the same room who've both personally seen the last Westley.'

We weren't going to make any more progress.

'A pleasure to meet you, but I'm a little tight on time,' I said. 'Thanks for the information. Maybe I'll take you up on that other offer some day.'

'Me, too.' Holland put down his glass.

'I have a dinner engagement, and my wife promised me her own particular brand of hell if I don't show. See you around, Nigel.'

He began to lead the way out. Bravington said 'I won't keep you Josh. I certainly don't want Moira round here on the warpath.' Then he put a hand on my arm. 'Mark, I'd appreciate it if you could stay just a few minutes. Please.'

I hesitated.

'Sure, you stay if you want,' breezed Holland. 'But I'm not kidding about that dinner party. I still have the scars from our last little misunderstanding. Keep in touch, Preston.'

It seemed to be decided. Holland was already halfway through the door, and I was still standing there.

'Look, I'm not giving you a rush act about what a busy man I am.' I explained. 'The fact is, I have a lot of people to see before this day is over.'

'I'll be as quick as I can. We can't talk here, there are too many people who'd consider life incomplete if they didn't interrupt. I have private rooms upstairs. This way.'

It was probably a waste of time. But I couldn't just walk out on the guy, after Holland had taken the trouble to bring me. There was also just a remote possibility that this was all a big sham, this business about there being no copies of the Judith painting. That was how I was coming to think of it. The Judith painting. Maybe this Bravington would come on strong with some elaborate yarn about not being able to speak freely in front of Holland. Because the fact is you see, Preston, I happen to know where there's a copy. No one else knows about it. It's the only one in existence. — It always is — . You are obviously so interested that I felt I must tell you, but the price, I'm afraid is, well — astronomical.

Then I would get all hot and excited, knowing the copy existed, the only one of its kind. Within an hour I'd be hocking the ranch, the car, even the forget-me-not bracelet handed down from dear old great-grandmama.

This is the kind of thinking I was doing

as I followed Bravington to the spiral metal staircase in the corner.

'Hey, Nigel, you walking out on us?'

One of the youngsters called after him plaintively, and the others made a chorus of catcalls. With a foot on the first rung, he smiled at them brilliantly.

'Now, now, my pretties. This is a teeny matter of business. Poor Nigel has to soil his hands with that nasty old bread every now and then, so he can keep strong and active for the important things in life. And you know what those are.'

He smiled obscenely and I felt revulsion. Not so the fan club. They thought he was great.

'Hurry back, sweetie' and

'Are you safe going up first, dear.'

And stuff like that. Nigel minced upwards, giving his rear end plenty of action. I couldn't figure it. A few minutes ago, he'd been quite a normal character. Now he seemed to be doing his audition for the Queer of the Year show. One of the Nigels was a phoney. Which one?

There were two rooms upstairs, made private by a door at the head of the staircase which he shut firmly once we were through. No pink up here, no drapes. Just plain wooden furniture, a big chesterfield, hi-fi layout, a small television. Far from being ornate, the place was austere. The other room was a kitchen.

'Sit down, Mark, sit down. I won't be a minute.'

I plonked down on a chair that was more comfortable than it looked, and gave my attention to the room's one decoration. It was a painting, of a man. He looked anywhere between thirty and forty years old, with a handsome, lean face, spoiled by a sardonic set to the full mouth. The black hair was thick and unruly above pale blue eyes, which seemed to bore into the spectator. The whole thing was compelling, making it a positive action to tear the eyes away and look elsewhere.

I heard Bravington moving around in the kitchen. Then the noise stopped.

'Mark.'

The voice came from the doorway. I excused myself mentally from the man on the wall and turned towards the voice.

Guns come in many shapes and sizes, because they serve many different purposes.

This one was shaped with rounded sides. That made it a revolver. It was very big, not to say huge. That made it at least a .44 caliber if not a .45. Whatever its original purpose, the present one was clear. It was pointed at my head.

Nigel said 'I think there are things you forgot to tell me.'

5

I stared into the dull gleam of the barrel,
knowing what a thing that size could do
to me at such short range. I looked above
it, to the man in charge. He was all cold
implacable purpose. If this was his way of
setting me up for a con over the picture, it
was certainly original. But it didn't make
sense.

'I don't get it,' I told him.

His face was thoughtful.

'Good. Your reaction already tells me
something I didn't know. Most people
would have a fit, or go down on their
knees, or sweat. They'd do something.
Not you. That makes you a man who's
not looking at his first gun.'

I shrugged.

'So you learned something. Now you
can put the howitzer back in the toybox,
and we can have our conversation.'

That made him puzzled.

'And that's all?'

84

'That's all,' I assured him.

That's all, unless you wanted to include the fact that I was scared as hell.

'You have to look at it from my angle,' I reasoned. 'Why the gun? What's it for? I didn't insult the family name. I didn't run off with your wife. I didn't break in here, you brought me. You don't have a reason to kill me. Of course, it's always possible you're one of those homicidal maniacs we read about. But I don't think so. Josh Holland would never introduce me to one of those.'

The gun had been wavering from its original true, deadly line. Now, it dropped to his side. He passed his free hand over his face. I was very careful not to move. For all my calm reasoning, I wasn't about to forget the golden rule. The guy with the gun is always the guy with the gun. Suddenly, he groaned. A low, suffering sound.

'I must be losing my mind.'

There was no answer to that, and I didn't offer one.

Now he shambled, rather than walked, across to a chair opposite me and sank down heavily. The huge gun dangled a few inches above the carpeted floor. The only sound in the room was the noisy ticking of an old-fashioned metal alarm clock. I waited. Finally, the fair head straightened and he looked over.

'What do you know about me?'

'Nothing,' I assured him. 'Sorry if it hurts your pride, but I never heard of you till an hour ago. You're probably famous, and all that, but this isn't my world. I just have a visitor's ticket.'

He listened closely.

'But Holland brought you here. He must have told you something about me?'

It sounded like a hurt pride situation, but there had to be more.

'As soon as I told him what I wanted, he said you were the man I had to see. Just like that. Not a word more.'

'Christ.'

He stood up suddenly. I stiffened in my chair. With only five feet between us, there was nothing else to be done. There was nothing on his face to indicate what he might be going to do next.

'Here.'

His arm straightened, and the gun sailed through the air between us. I caught it gratefully. And I'd been right. It was a .45.

'You'd better call the police, I guess. There's a phone behind you, on the table.'

I sat still, quite happy just cuddling my new toy.

'Police?' I echoed. 'What for?'

He sat down again, suddenly shapeless.

'I don't know,' he replied dully. 'Attempted murder, assault with a deadly weapon. Something. There has to be something.'

I would go along with that. And I was far too interested to learn what that something might be to be wasting my time calling for the law.

'Probably,' I agreed. 'But let's not bother with it. You made an error of judgement, the way I see it. If we're going to start locking up all the people who do that, who'll deliver the milk?'

That brought me a faint grin.

'You're an odd one. Do you always

react this way when people try to kill you?'

'Not always. But I usually know the reason. What did you think was going to happen? Did you expect me to rob the vault, or something?'

He ran fingers through his hair, now dank and lifeless.

'I doubt if there's a hundred dollars in the place. Don't suppose you'd care to tell me who you are?'

'We already went through that.'

He waved an impatient arm.

'Not just your name. I mean, who are you? You've seen the Westley of the Rivers woman. That puts you into an unusual bracket, right off.'

I recoiled mentally from the description of Judith as being the Rivers woman. Even as I did so, I knew I was being childish.

'Yes, so I hear. But I'd no idea at the time. I thought her husband was just being a little over-anxious about the sunlight attacking the paint. It seems I was wrong.'

'You still didn't tell me who you are.'

88

I tapped the blue metal resting on my lap.

'You still didn't tell me why you waved this under my nose. And I don't want to turn nasty, but there is such a thing as assault with a deadly weapon.'

'O.K.'

He got up again. It's very disconcerting, sitting in a room with a guy who bobs up and down like a jack-in-the-box.

'I'm going to tell you what made me behave that way. But first I'm going to have a drink. How about you?'

'If you're going back in that kitchen, how do I know you won't come back with a Thompson?'

'Thompson?'

'It's a sub-machine gun,' I explained.

'Oh,' and again the small grin. 'No, I cleared them all away. Didn't have the space. There's Scotch.'

'Scotch'll be fine.'

I found myself drawn again to look at the picture on the wall. The man stared back, with the same kind of aloof amusement as before. He'd taken the whole thing in his stride, the gun-waving, the threats. It was as though the antics of lesser people were to be taken no more seriously than the movement of ants on a garden path. You'd think he could have shown some concern or relief. Something. Anything but the cool appraisal he was giving me.

'You seem to like the picture.'

Bravington stood above me, holding out a glass.

'Thanks.'

I took it from him, making the ice clink.

'I don't think we'd get along,' I told him. 'The guy is too damned self-contained by half.'

He sat back down where he'd been before. I hoped he'd stay the course a little better. Maybe a full minute, for example.

'It's him I want to talk about. Partly, that is. Douglas.'

'Douglas?' I repeated. 'Westley, right. You're telling me that's Douglas Westley?'

He nodded.

'I am. And you're wrong, you know. You and he would have got along just fine. The way you handled that gun business just now, that was exactly how he would have behaved, I'm sure of it. The dialogue may have differed, but the attitude would have been the same.'

'H'm.'

I looked back at the man who was not to be thought of as Westley, and knew the speaker was right. I'd have liked to ask more about him, but first I wanted to hear Bravington's story.

'Good Scotch,' I acknowledged. 'Do we talk now?'

'We do. I'm sorry you never heard of me. That means I'll have to tell you myself. So I'll start with a disclaimer. I'm not talking just to impress you. But it would be wrong for me to be too modest, if you're to understand things. You see, you were quite right the first time. I am famous, in my own little world. Douglas Westley only ever had three pupils. I am the one who made it. First, as his most promising find, then as the acknowledged expert on his work. Lastly, and only after years of living in his shadow, as an original in my own right. Not the

91

promising pupil, not the second Westley, but the first Bravington. It took a long time.'

He stopped for a moment.

'Do you resent it?' I queried. 'And him?'

I waved a glass towards the picture. He grinned.

'Resent him? Douglas? Oh no, you don't have the right idea at all. I loved that man.'

There must have been some reaction on my face, without my knowing it.

'No, and you have the wrong idea there too. I'm not talking about some fag worship. I'm talking about the kind of deep respect, admiration, affection a man can have for another man without it being sexual. Any of that, and Douglas would have heaved me out on my ear.'

'He sounds like a helluva man.'

'Right.' He seemed to withdraw into his own thoughts for a while. Then, 'In a way, it ties in with what I did a moment ago. Funny, you can go along thinking that the past is the past, then up comes something to remind you. To bring it all back to life, fresh as ever. That's what happened downstairs, when Josh Holland said you'd seen her picture. Everything came back.'

It was irritating, the way he would stop, just when I was about to learn something.

'I don't see it yet,' I jogged. 'Looking at paintings is no kind of crime. It isn't even a social offence. If I'm wrong, we're going to need bigger jails.'

'Sorry. I'm wandering. First, you have to know about him.' He pointed to the man on the wall. 'I don't know what it takes to make a genius. The word gets bandied around too much. Every third-rater who failed as an artist gets himself a column in some provincial rag. Then he holds forth about all the things he can't do, only now he's an expert. And he has to produce an average of one genius per year, otherwise the customers feel they're not getting their money's worth. You know the kind of crap. 'This shining new talent' and so forth. If enough of them share the same view, it begins to be possible they really are on to something. Or someone, more precisely. Many years ago, they all latched on to Douglas

Westley, and he took off. The genius with the flaw. That's what they called him.'

He looked at me for some kind of recognition. I shook my head.

'Flaw?' I queried. 'What does it mean?'

'He concentrated on portraits. That's where his strength was. He'd tried other things, many others. They showed him to be a good, reliable craftsman. Nothing else. No better than dozens of others, maybe hundreds. He hadn't found his field. Once he did, there was no holding him. He was bold, incisive. The pictures glittered like cut crystal.

'But with a flaw,' I persisted.

Bravington shrugged, and sipped at his drink.

'Honesty. That was what they chose to call a flaw. We are none of us perfect, as people. There's always a side to every-one's nature, some characteristic, that makes a man less than perfect. No matter who he is. An archbishop, a president, anyone. When Douglas produced a work, somehow or other a hint of this would creep in. He couldn't help it. A lot of so-called painters don't produce paintings at all. What they give you is a photograph done with brushes and oils. An expensive studio photograph, with the lighting just right, all the most flattering features emphasised.'

'But that's what people want, surely? Nobody wants to look as though he just rolled home from a three-day party.'

The glass was empty now, and he set it down with a flourish.

'You're taking the other extreme. I don't mean that. Douglas would paint like anybody else, flattery and all. Almost a photograph in fact. But it was as though he photographed the soul. As though the paint went right through the man's skin and found his heart. Nothing dramatic would emerge. It would be no more than a faint line in one case. The mere suggestion of a shadow in another. You'd have to search to find it. But it would be there. Somewhere.'

The reason I was so interested was personal, I admitted to myself. With annoyance. There was something I'd missed on Judith's picture. Correction. On the portrait of the Rivers woman.

Still, as my lecturer was explaining, it wouldn't leap to the eye. You had to search for it. I was wondering how soon I could persuade Rivers to let me see the portrait again.'

'About the Judith Harvey Rivers picture,' I prompted.

'Sorry, yes. I was wandering away again. My favourite subject, as you may have gathered.'

'I had noted more than a passing interest,' I told him.

He really was quite a good-looking guy when he smiled.

'Douglas used to let people think he was queer. Did you know about that?'

A switch, if you like.

'No. Nobody mentioned it.'

'Well, he did. There are people around who seem to expect it, you know. Even the straights expect it. You saw that bunch, down there, just now. Have to do a little acting myself, sometimes.'

'I've known legit actors do the same,' I contributed.

'Part of the scene. Douglas used to laugh about it, when we were alone. Had his own name for himself. The fag with a flaw. His flaw was that he liked women. Liked them?' he repeated. 'What am I saying? He was crazy for them. If he hadn't been a painter, he'd have made all-American stud.'

'Couldn't have been easy to find the opportunities, I imagine? I mean, if everybody thinks you button your jacket the wrong side — '

'But that was how he did it. Brilliant. He let them reform him. How could they resist? He'd tell them how they'd changed his life. How he'd missed out, in his youth. He'd never met a woman who didn't revolt him. And now, suddenly, here she was. The perfection he'd always heard about, but never found. Oh, the wasted years, the loneliness. Believe me, you mentioned actors just now. Not many could have compared to him, once he was on the bedpath. They fell over like ten-pins. The woman felt it was practically a sacred duty, you see. A chance to bring this poor creature back into the heterosexual world. It was nothing to do with the bed-scene. They were reclaiming a man on behalf of all womankind. Some of them even tried to instruct him. Ye gods.'

I couldn't resist a chuckle, not only at the original technique of Douglas Westley, but at the admiring respect in his one-time pupil's tone.

'He certainly seems to have had a new method of dealing with a very old problem.'

'Right. It was amazing how he got away with it. Year after year, and no kickbacks. Of course, it had to come to an end sometime. And the end was that lady who brought you here. Judith Harvey Rivers.'

I misunderstood him entirely. Naturally it had to end with Judith. It would take more than some brass-balled guy with a paintbrush to impress a woman like that.

'She turned him down flat, huh?'

Bravington's eyes widened in amazed denial.

'Turned him down?' he repeated. 'She was wild about him. Besotted. Absolutely mad-crazy. That's why she killed him.'

6

The metal of the revolver felt very cold against my hand. The hand that wanted to thrash out and punch hell out of his stupid, lying face. What was the matter with me?

My voice sounded strangely thick as I said

'Killed him? Am I hearing you right?'

He was quick to sense my change of attitude, as his face showed.

'What else? Oh, I know all the history, the stuff the papers gave out. Douglas committed suicide and all that. Not true. It was her. She killed him, and then a little while after she couldn't live with it. Went out into the bay and smashed herself up. In a way, she cheated me. I was going to wait till things cooled off. Then I was going to kill that lady myself. But she beat me to it.'

Bravington was obviously not balanced, I decided.

'That's a hell of an accusation. What did the police make of it?'

He sneered.

'Police? I never told them. What happened was this. When Douglas was killed, I was away. Down in Baja California middle of nowhere, trying to do a sunset. The usual thing. The setting sun down there does things with colour that you wouldn't believe. Everybody tries to capture it sometime during his career. Nobody ever succeeded, and I was no exception. But that's where I was, completely out of touch. When I came back, it was all over. They were both dead. I was drunk for three days. Drunk, and brooding about what to do. In the end I decided to say nothing. For Douglas' sake.'

That sounded false.

'I don't follow that. How would it help him, your keeping quiet?'

He brought out a pack of small cigars and lit one. He didn't offer the pack. It was my guess he could sense I would tell him what to do with it.

'As I said before, it was all over. The

media had decided to give him a decent burial. They didn't rake him over, which wouldn't have been too hard. They made him a kind of heroic figure, a genius who couldn't live with himself. A poor tortured soul who'd failed as a man. A brilliant painter whose work hung in every major gallery, and who would have made folk hero, except for that fatal weakness in his makeup. Every leading figure in the art-world had made his little speech, written a little obituary. The whole thing was wrapped up. Can you imagine the reaction from all those people, and the world at large, if I'd come along and said it was all bunk? And even if I finally managed to convince anybody, where would it leave Douglas? The tortured genius who was really bumped off by an angry dame. All the praise would have been re-assessed. People don't like that. Don't like going back on public statements. The result would have been to damage him. I didn't want that. And of course, you have to remember it wouldn't have served any purpose. Nobody was getting away with anything.

The woman was already dead herself.'

'H'm.'

Since I wasn't being included in the cigars, I pulled out my Old Favourites and lit one. It tasted sour. Like Bravington's story.

'I think you left out something,' I told him. 'You left out the part about it wouldn't have helped the living at all.'

'The living?' His brow creased up. 'Her husband? I didn't give one damn what happened to him.'

That I believed. But I still shook my head.

'Not the husband, Nigel. You.'

'Me?'

'Right. You were on your way. Brilliant pupil, now making it on your own. A man in that spot would have to be a first-class chump to make monkeys out of all the people whose good opinion he needed. And a chump you ain't.'

Whatever else, I added to myself.

'You're right, of course.' He hung his head. 'Somewhere along the line, in the middle of all that noble purpose, there was me. Nothing would bring Douglas

Westley back. Nothing would even add to his reputation, or the memory of him. There was nothing to be gained. And, as you say, I had an entire career to lose.'

He sounded sad and far away. Full of self-recrimination. I tapped at the forty-five.

'That still doesn't explain this,' I reminded.

But he wasn't very interested any more. He'd stirred up too much of the memory-mud. In a tired kind of voice he said.

'After I'd calmed down, I went out there to the house. I was certain Rivers must have known the truth. About Douglas and his wife, I mean. Whatever Judith Rivers may have been, she was certainly no routine criminal. She wouldn't know how to commit murder, and make it look like suicide. In any case, people who kill in a blind rage don't even think about things like that. The first thing they know, they're standing over a body, not quite certain how it got there.'

That made a lot more sense than most

people would know. I was paying careful attention.

'So?'

'So, what was I to make of it? The murder squad in this city have a very high reputation. You don't fool those guys too easily. And with a prominent corpse like Douglas, they would be looking with great care. They'd have hollered murder inside twenty-four hours. Somebody made it look otherwise. And not Judith. Not a hot-tempered woman, full of remorse and fear, and everything that goes with a situation like that. No, somebody else did. Some remote, cold-hearted bastard, who could approach the problem in a detached and clinical way. Somebody who could pay for what needed to be done. That somebody was your buddy, Bernard L. Rivers.'

I thought if I didn't contradict him, I might learn something.

'So you went to see him.'

'Huh.'

His face wreathed in disgust at the recollection.

'Oh yes, I saw him. He sat behind that

big desk, and he heard me out. For all the reaction I got you'd have thought I was propositioning the guy on an insurance deal. He didn't interrupt me once. Just sat there, staring. I can see his face now. When I was finished he took me to pieces, like a guy with a dead mouse in a laboratory. He didn't even raise his voice, you know that? Told me I was upset, and it was quite natural. My faggot friend was dead, and I was like any woman who'd lost a man. Judith had been the Purity Queen of that and every other year. I'd better take my sick mind away and have a long think. His wife was dead, and he'd suffered all he intended to. Told me, if I tried to do anything to discredit her memory, he would spend every last dollar he had to ruin me. As for the picture, the last one Douglas ever finished, he, Rivers, hated it. He was going to wait his time, before he did anything about it. If he sold it then, or if anything happened to it, a lot more public attention would be attracted than would normally happen. The two principals were newly dead. So he would do nothing, until the time was ripe.'

'I see.'

I thought about that for a few moments, trying to follow his reasoning.

'And then, just now, when I came in here, you decided that was Rivers' way of letting you know he was going to sell the picture?'

'Or destroy it,' he nodded. 'Far more likely, is my guess.'

Mine too, after what he'd told me. But I didn't think it would be a good idea to let him know that.

'I think I understand that. Especially with me asking if there are copies. A man who intends to dispose of an original would naturally look around for copies.'

Bravington listened to me, with his fair head cocked to one side.

'You still haven't contradicted me,' he pointed out.

I got up from the chair.

'What happened is exactly what I told you in the first place,' I assured him. 'I'm just a man who saw a pretty picture and wants one for himself. By way of an answer I get this thing stuck in my face, and twenty minutes of all this True

106

Detective. Is it always this tough to buy something around here?'

Shaken though he still was, he contrived a small grin.

'I'm sorry. I really am sorry. Just take it that I'm descended from a long line of patent medicine travellers. A story with every bottle. But I still don't have your mixture. There are no copies.'

I handed him the gun, barrel first.

'Here. You'll need this for the next customer.'

He took it sheepishly, and put it down on a table.

We walked to the door.

'I'll see myself down.'

We were relaxed now, the tension past. A good time to slug a man. Swinging round suddenly, I stared into his eyes.

'Do you have any cut-up newspapers I could buy?'

Nothing. Not surprise, not fear. Not even the quick blank veil some people can pull. Just astonishment.

'Newspapers? How do you mean, for a collage or something like that? Out of my line, Mark. This art-dealer stuff is not my line of country at all. I could give you a guy's name — '

'No, don't bother. It was just a passing thought.'

Down in the pink room, the high school crowd stopped chattering long enough to dissect me as I passed through on my way out.

★ ★ ★

I drove around to the offices of the Monkton City Globe, deep in thought. The night staff would be just reporting in, ready for the steady grind through the dark hours so that Mr and Mrs Monkton would be sure of a steady mixture of romance and horror and crime and sex and disaster and sport and you name it. All set out neat and tidy, alongside the breakfast cereal.

The night editor is an old friend of mine, Shad Steiner. Thirty years at the trade have brought him every kind of accolade, all well deserved. But he never changes, never gives any sign of mellowing into the old pro, the kind-hearted father figure, doling out spoonfuls of wisdom to the eager young faces of the cub reporters. He's still the same irascible, suspicious, hate-all character he was when he started. That's what made him a great newspaperman in the first place, and that's what keeps him right up there with the winners. That, and one or two side-effects. Like honesty, integrity, and some other of those outdated words which only appear in very old dictionaries.

He was standing in front of a desk heaped with piles of paper of varying heights. The rapidly enlarging bald area on top of his head gleamed with early perspiration, as if in anticipatory dread of the sweating hours which would now inevitably follow. He could sense there was someone behind him, but he didn't bother to check who it was before he said.

'Some day, I'm just not going to bother about going home after work. I'm going to stay out and swing the day shift as well. Show these bums something about running a newspaper. Especially, I'm going to show them the way to leave the fixings for the night editor to pick up. I mean, look at this garbage here. Is that any kind of mess to find when a man reports for work? Wouldn't you think a man's pride would force him to leave the desk in what the politicians call some semblance of order? Just drop your stuff in the middle there. I'll get to it when I can.'

He pointed a thick, nail-bitten finger vaguely towards the piles. I made my voice eager.

'Let me take a crack at it, chief. Just gimme a break. Some day I'm gonna be a great newspaper man. Just like you, Mr Steiner.'

He stiffened, turning.

'Listen, you — oh. Oh, very funny. You're Preston, right? And you need a job. Sorry, I already have people covering the morgues.'

'Hallo Shad, business as usual, huh?'

He was shrugging off his jacket now, and draping it crookedly over a peg on the wall.

'Business is, as usual, being interrupted by every bum who wanders in off the

110

street,' he growled. 'This here is a newspaper office, you know. Not a soup kitchen. You need a handout, you go down to Crane Street, and — '

'I know the place,' I assured him. 'I researched it out, so I'll know where to find you after the Globe gets wise to you, and gives you the heave.'

'So we'll meet later. Now, if you'll excuse me, just for the next few years — . Or did you want something?'

I leaned up against a corner, close to a picture of a younger Steiner shaking hands with a former President.

'Almost nothing,' I assured him. 'A little poke around in the old dusty files. Nothing to worry about.'

'So it is a handout,' he said triumphantly. 'And don't tell me what I should worry about. I do my own worrying. You know when I get worried most? When some expensive private policeman goes poking around in my morgue, and telling me not to worry. That's when I worry. You're most likely about to reveal the crime of the century, and you won't even tell an old buddy, who's been like a father to you all these years. Is this the thanks I get?'

'Shad, if there's a story, you get it. I doubt if it'll run, personally. Just some old stuff that happened a few years back. May help me to understand what's happening now.'

He opened a drawer where he kept his blue marking pencils, drew one out and chewed on the end.

'What was it all about, this boring tale that I don't have to worry about?'

'Tragic death of society beauty. Sea claims fresh victim. Her name was Judith Harvey Rivers.'

I thought if I spoke in headlines, he could follow me more easily.

'That one,' he recalled. 'Her old man was Rivers, some kind of bullion king?'

'That one,' I confirmed. 'Just a passing interest, to tell the truth. She had her picture painted, just before she died. By Douglas Westley, no less. That makes it a lot of picture, very expensive. That's the part I'm really looking into. May be an insurance angle coming up. I told you it was dull.'

The engraved lines on his face etched themselves further in.

'Society beauties, famous painters, sudden death,' he repeated. 'These things are dull to you? I was right not to give you a job. You'd never make reporter. What kind of stuff would you consider interesting? World War Three, maybe?'

The trouble with a man like Steiner, his nose is always ready to twitch, the ink waiting to pound through his veins.

'Yesterday's news,' I reminded him. 'There's nothing exciting about dusting off old corpses. The kind of thing I'm looking into might rate six lines on page ten. If it does, I'll put it your way.'

'Now he lays out the edition for me.' He put his head back, in entreaty to the great publisher in the sky. 'Well, I'll just have to take your word. Got to get on with the rest of the pages. Give you a break, though.'

It was my turn to be suspicious.

'A break?' I queried.

The bald head flashed light as he waved it up and down.

'Somebody here who can maybe fill in

a little background for you. Should be finishing work right now, being one of these dayshift stars, but probably won't object to giving you a few minutes.'

He picked up a telephone and dialled.

'Mike? Steiner. No, I didn't, not yet. The city refuse department emptied a truck on my desk. I'm sending out for a shovel, it's bound to be under here someplace. Sure, when I find it. Listen, there's a guy with — '

He droned, telling the unseen Mike what I wanted.

' — and there's probably nothing in it, at all. Still, you never know. This Preston has tossed one or two pieces our way, over the years. If you wouldn't mind just giving him a minute or two — . Yeah. Thanks Mike. A favour. Do the same.'

The phone banged down.

'You're in luck. Fourth cubicle down on the left. Society Editor. Name is Mike Blair. I think you'll get along just fine.'

Somewhere in those recessed eyes was a laugh. Something phoney about this Blair, I decided. Keeping suspicion from my voice, I said 'I'm obliged, Shad. If anything comes of this, I'll see you get it.'

'Good. Anyway, I'm sure Mike'll look after the Globe interests.'

Puzzled, I went down the corridor to the fourth door, and knocked. I went inside, and looked into wide hazel eyes, framed by tumbling hair the colour of a tropic night. Red lips parted in a smile as she said

'Mr Preston? I'm Mike Blair.'

7

She stood up to shake hands, and became tall. Five eight, five nine maybe. I squared my shoulders and pulled in my spine to let her see I was taller. The movement, as they say, did not go unnoticed.

'The procedure is to shake firmly but briefly, then let go. I hadn't intended to make you a present of it.'

She was talking about the hand I was holding with loving care. I laughed unconvincingly, and let it go with reluctance.

'Hobby of mine,' I explained. 'You'd be surprised how many I get to keep that way.'

The grin was faint, but a very attractive addition to the tanned, almost olive skin.

'Please sit down, Mr Preston.'

'Mark, please,' I almost begged. 'If you were a man, I'd call you Mike. The fact that you're one of the other kind ought not to stand in the way. Mike and Mark.

Sounds good, don't you think?'

'It sounds terrible,' she assured me gravely. 'Like some ancient vaudeville act. Besides, what would we call the children?'

A suitable point at which to switch subjects.

'Miss Blair — '

'I thought we agreed on Mike?'

'Mike, then. Shad Steiner gave you a rough idea of what I'm looking for. Do you recall any of the circumstances?'

She clasped her hands together beneath her chin.

'Shad gave me a rough idea, as you say. What he didn't tell me was why the famous Mr Preston should be interested.'

Her tone wasn't all mockery.

'Famous?' I hedged. 'What's with the famous?'

'Sole survivor — well almost — of the famous Gunfight at Monkton Corral. I'd call that fame. Of a kind.'

'Gunfight at — oh, you mean that thing at the railroad yards.[1] I wouldn't have thought you'd read the crime pages.'

---

[1] The Day of the Big Dollar

'Avidly,' she assured me. 'Well, why are you interested?'

I made a gesture of dismissal.

'Don't get the wrong impression. Reporters, well crime beat guys anyway, they tend to romanticise now and then. Being an investigator is mostly very dull work, believe me. Like now.'

It didn't go over the way I'd intended.

'I must be sure not to detain you in our dull surroundings for too long.'

She was playing with me now. The eyes told me.

'You know I didn't mean that the way it sounded. The fact is this is a routine enquiry. Douglas Westley's last completed work was a portrait of Judith Harvey Rivers deceased. I've become interested in both of them. Like to read the old coverage, and pick up anything else I can. Stuff that didn't reach the public. It's no more complicated than that, believe me.'

'Uh, huh. Well, you've come to the right girl. I was new on the paper when all this happened. It seemed a good opportunity to dig into things from the woman's angle. I'm talking mainly about the Rivers death, of course. Where did she buy her clothes, how much jewellery did she use, that kind of thing. I learned a lot about her.'

She stopped talking. I couldn't decide whether she was gathering her thoughts or inviting questions.

'Did you like her?'

I blurted it out almost unintentionally. It brought the reaction it deserved. Mike Blair arched her eyebrows in a question.

'Like her? What kind of question is that? I never met the woman.'

But I'd recovered myself now. There'd been a moment at which I'd have explained that it was important to me to know what people thought about Judith. That I was hungry for information that would round out my picture of her. Give support to all the good things that were plain to see on that face. Get rid of any nagging worries planted by Nigel Bravington, with all that stuff about a character defect being painted there, once you studied the picture closely. I didn't want to hear that kind of thing. I wanted only to hear good things, things that gave weight to the opinion I was anxious to have. Mike watched me thinking, and wondered.

'No, no of course you didn't. But all I meant was, some general impression. Which side would she line up? With the good guys, or the bad guys?'

'Ah.' She opened a sandalwood box on the desk, and turned it towards me. It was filled with fat black cigarets. I took one gingerly, sniffing at it. Mike picked up a chunky table-lighter and held it out. 'Stop looking so suspicious. They're quite straightforward. Marijuana one end, straight opium the other.'

I grinned sheepishly and held it in the flame. It wasn't bad, maybe a little too sweet. She lit one herself, and threw back her head to blow smoke around. An old actress trick, but it does command the attention, which is why they do it. Which is why she did it. My attention was properly commanded.

'Did I like her?' She appeared to be asking herself. 'Which side would she stand? With the good guys, I would say. You know, or if you don't know you'll at least understand, that a rich woman is up against a lot of unspoken hostility, before she starts. Mrs Mainstreet can be bitchy, occasionally bad-tempered, given to the screams, and people will allow for it. I'm speaking of other women when I say people.'

She looked at me directly.

'Oh sure,' I agreed. 'Lots of women are people. I've met a number myself.'

'I'll bet. That's Mrs Mainstreet. Mrs Nob-Hill has no such allowances made. The money gives two strikes against her right off. To be counted with the good guys, she has to be a whole lot nicer than almost anybody else.'

I warmed to this Mike Blair. A woman of judgement, that was plain to be seen. One who was able to classify Judith Harvey Rivers correctly. A good guy. But she hadn't finished.

'Right up until the time she died. She lost a lot of points then. With me, anyway.'

'I don't follow that.'

'She had no business out in the bay, driving around like a mad thing. There

121

was more than just her own life to think about, but she couldn't have cared very much. The lady was three months pregnant.'

'Ah.'

It wasn't a very intelligent contribution, but it was all I could muster while I absorbed this new information.

'That would influence your assessment, of course.'

'Of course.'

I knew I was pushing too hard, showing too much interest in what I was claiming to be background information. It was time to move on to something else.

'What about the other case. The painter, Westley. Did you spend any time on him?'

The provocative mouth curled disdainfully.

'No. There wouldn't be anything there for me. My readers are not exactly consumed with interest in fag painters.'

'No, I can see that. Well, I'm obliged to you, Mike. And especially for staying after work.'

She inclined the immaculate head in

acknowledgement.

'My pleasure. Anyway, I couldn't resist the opportunity of meeting the notorious gunfighter. I really ought to go now. At this time of day I normally meet a few people for a quick drink on my way home.'

Drink. And then home. It sounded like a first-class sequence to me. But it would have to be some other night.

'Another time I'd have been begging you to take me along,' I assured her. 'Tonight, I work. Including the whole night. Could I just go down and take a quick peek at the files on these two, before I go?'

She shrugged.

'Help yourself. I'm sure you know the way.'

We got up, grinding out our cigarettes at the same time. I liked being close to her.

'I was wondering whether I might call you some time?'

'We're in the classifieds. Under Newspapers and Magazines. Lots of people call in.'

Ouch.

'I could give you an exclusive on the confessions of a gunslinger,' I persisted.

She relented a little. Enough to smile, at least.

'We'll see. There's no harm in your trying, after all.'

At the door she turned right to go out. I went left, for the stairs down to the great filing system known as the morgue. Before descending, I looked around to watch the tall supple figure going away from me. She was quickly gone.

I wrenched my mind away from the living, and concentrated on the dead. The file on Judith Harvey Rivers was thin, apart from the reports on her death. Reportage on her career as an actress was confined to a few lines only, and I could understand that. In my town, to qualify as an actress you have to be known on the small screen. Five seasons of Shakespeare on the legitimate stage is nowhere. Not when you compare it with a weekly stint as the friendly hash slinger in the Fighting Sheriff Thompson series. Or even a soap ad. Unless she appears on television,

124

there's only two other places for people calling themselves actresses. The burlesque theatre, and the streets. But I read what there was with great care. It was as though the yellowing printed clips were giving me a chance to get close to her, to know her. The pictures did her no justice at all. They were just flat black and white shots of a good-looking woman. There was no way of detecting the warm radiance that exuded from behind those steel shutters out at Rivers Bend.

I didn't care for the style of reporting, either. Flat, and emotionless stuff. Just a lot of bleak facts, set out in stark columns. None of the humanity which any fool should know to be essential to a proper understanding of the woman who died. But I stuck to it, every word.

When I replaced the file, the identification tab on the next one caught my eye. Rivers, Laurence. There were two items in there. One was a report on a drunk driving charge. Larry Rivers drew fifty dollars and a warning on that one. The other made me sit up. A paternity suit had been made against him by a girl named Patti Dean, 18, a fellow student at the Monkton School for the Arts. It seemed to have been the usual messy kind of case, a lot of mud being thrown, without much of it sticking. The girl had lost the case, and the date-line announced it had been a little over a year ago.

On impulse, I raked around to see what else there was to be known about Dean, Patti. There was a folder, with repeat items about the court case. But also there was a more recent picture, of a smiling young girl waving at the camera man. The headline said 'Smiling winner leaves'. It seemed the smiling winner had been awarded a special scholarship to spend one year researching into Aztec art. There was no reference to any baby, or to the earlier case involving Larry Rivers. The scholarship was a new one, it said, founded by the benevolence of the giant Transcontinental Metal. The only metal I knew that connected with the Aztecs was gold.

Telling myself not to be so dramatic about these remote connections, I still went to the business section of the file

126

system, and looked out the company. Transcontinental was what the Globe said it was. A giant outfit, to put it mildly. The membership of the board was not unlike a quick fingering through Who's Who. And right there, among the Who's who were Who, was nobody but my old buddy, Bernard L. Rivers.

I argued with myself.

'A coincidence. The guy is probably on the board of half the companies on the Coast.'

'Maybe. But if we look at the people who won those scholarships, how many will we find who were mixed up in unpleasant court cases with the families of the members of the board?'

'You know I can't answer that.'

'That's right, you can't. And here's another one you can't answer. If you were on the board, wouldn't you make it your business to see that people who attacked your family were not given scholarships?'

'He may not have known about it. He bakes a lot of pies. He can't keep up with every detail of routine.'

'Right. But this wasn't routine. This

was a new scheme. It says so right there. Everybody would be interested in how it came out. Who was to be the lucky winner.'

Back and forth it went in my mind. Try as I might, I could not shake the feeling that the girl had been got rid of. Bernard L. Rivers was a man who liked everything tidy, that much I knew. How far he'd push it was anybody's guess. But the girl had been involved with his son. There's been a public scandal. And now the girl was neatly out of the way.

It was time to stop the theorising, and get back to facts. Facts like the file on Douglas Westley.

He'd had a lot of coverage in the three or four years prior to his death. There were several photographs, all of which told me what an excellent painting it was that I'd seen hanging on the wall in Nigel Bravington's place. Westley seemed to have had the knack of keeping on the right side of the press. The artistic side was played up, the private life given plenty of soft pedal. Even so, the references to his clothes, mannerisms, and the kind of furnishings in his apartment left little room for doubt as to the man's homosexuality. If Bravington had been telling the truth, his one-time master had done a great cover-up job.

The truth, I sighed, turning over the clippings. If everybody spent more time telling the truth, I'd soon be out of a job.

The artist's suicide had been a fairly straightforward affair. He blew a hole in his heart, powder burns and all. At the inquest, I noted the investigating officer had been Detective Third Grade Schultz. Schultzie was one of John Rourke's officers, from the Homicide Bureau. A smart and reliable copper, well able to tell the difference between suicide and murder.

I closed the drawer, and checked my watch. Time to be getting out to the house.

8

On the road out, I passed the unpaved single track road with a sign saying 'City Reservoir', and recalled how my eyes had been drawn by that gleaming stretch of water when I looked out from the Rivers house. Although the reservoir had been quite close, looking across country, the approach road was several miles away, because of the windings of the highway.

As I reached the final curve, the one that brought Rivers Bend into view, I saw a Lincoln parked at the roadside. Leaning on the bonnet, watching my approach, was Sam Thompson.

I pulled over behind him, stopped and got out.

'Been waiting for you,' he greeted, unnecessarily. 'Nice evening, ain't it?'

'I thought we agreed to meet at the house?' I countered.

'Yeah, well, I get kind of shy around strangers. Don't like meeting new people.

Besides, I wanted to talk to you. You got a butt?'

But I'd already catered for that. When the list is compiled of the great cigarette-scroungers of history, Sam Thompson will be up there with the front runners. I handed him a fresh pack.

'Keep 'em. What did you want to talk about?'

He pushed a smoke into his face, and started patting around for matches. I sighed and held out my lighter. He took it, made flame, and was about to slip it into his pocket, but I tapped him on the arm, and he passed it back.

'It's about your buddy, Dr Franklyn Hoskins. A very interesting man.'

'Well?'

'Well, he's the real article all right. He didn't got his diploma from no barber's college. Went clear through medical school, did a shift as intern in one of the big New York hospitals — '

'New York?' I interrupted. 'You're sure about that?'

Thompson looked aggrieved.

'Aw come on, Preston, this isn't my

first job. Sure I'm sure. Anyways, he was doing fine over there, then something must have happened. And don't ask me what kind of something, because I don't know. Whatever it was, he quit the big apple, and came out here. Opened up his sanatorium, for people with what they call nervous disorders. That's what they call 'em when you can pay the tab. When you can't, they call 'em other things. Either way, it means the patient is nuts.'

'When did all this happen?' I wanted to know.

'Can't be sure within a few months. Not enough time. But, say three years. Just roughly.'

It would roughly do. Dr Hoskins' decision to settle in our great state seemed to have coincided more or less with the Rivers family move.

'Did you happen to learn about these nervous disorders? I mean, are these people drug takers, alcoholics, that kind of thing?'

The craggy face moved from side to side.

'Naw. No bums. Not as far as I know.

They seem to be people who are short one or two marbles. Women mostly. Severe emotional stress, they call it. To me, it's still nuts.'

I decided I could live without Sam's brand of low-flying philosophy.

'Is it a big place he runs? I mean how many patients would he have at one time?'

'Not many. Six, maybe eight. I guess they'd have to pay through the nose, right? I mean, to run a joint like that, you'd almost need that number of staff.'

The same thought had already occurred to me.

'That's true. But maybe he has other patients. Outside patients. Does he run a surgery, do you know?'

'Well now, that's one of the things makes him interesting. He had a practice for a long while, but he ran it into the ground. It seems your pal the doctor can't stay away from the gee-gees. Spends more time with the racing sheets than the medical books. I wouldn't say he's costing the bookies any sleep, not if his place is anything to judge by.'

'You've seen it, then?'

'Sort of took a little ride out that way. You know the way those places are as a rule. Everything clean and shiny, so a man has to watch where he plants his feet. Dr Hoskins' joint is not like that. Not any more. You can see where it would have been, one time. Now, it's kind of neglected, you know what I mean? Nobody cuts the grass, there's weeds in the driveway, the place needs a lick of paint. Stuff like that.'

A neglected sanatorium, or any kind of place, means that the people who work there also tend to get sloppy. Details get overlooked, work programs fall behind. People can't be relied on to do what they're being paid to do. Such as, keeping an eye on Olivia Jayne Hart.

'Did you check his credit rating?'

Again that aggrieved look.

'They didn't give me this Junior G-man badge for nothing, you know,' he grumbled. 'Sure I checked it. And there was a funny thing. Hoskins' personal rating is rocky, to say the least. And yet,' he paused for effect, 'the credit standing of the sanatorium itself, weeds and all, is gold-plated. How do you figure that one?'

How I figured that one was not something I was about to divulge to Sam Thompson, or anyone else. Not yet.

'You said that was one of the things that made him interesting. Tell me about the others.'

'He started on the booze, a couple of months back. You don't need me to tell you, Preston, when a man hits those gee-gees, and they start kicking back, many a man reaches for a glass. Oldest story in the world. That, and women.'

Which was another question I'd been about to ask.

'Yes, how about women? Is he married, this Hoskins?'

'Not so far as I know. He could have been one time, back in those New York days, but I haven't been able to find out. You forget, I only had a few hours.'

I held up a hand, before he got properly launched.

'You're quite right, Sam. I do ask too much. You've done a lot in a very short time. We'd better get up to the house. Did you get the gun out of hock?'

He tapped at his middle.

'Back in position,' he confirmed.

I knew my next question would be unpopular.

'Is it loaded this time?'

His face became sad and reproachful.

'Now come on, Preston, everybody gets to make one mistake.'

'One is all you're allowed.'

There'd been a misunderstanding, a year or two earlier, about some money that went missing from a bank. One of the citizens who was being misunderstood started blasting away with a hand-gun. Sam Thompson was all set to misunderstand right back at him, because he had a gun too. Only, in his case, he'd forgotten to load it. He collected one in the neck, and one in the side, and was on the danger list for four days, before they straightened him out.

'And the blanket-rolls?'

He nodded, and groaned.

'I hate this job already.'

'Just think about the money. It helps to concentrate the mind.'

We'd been strolling along the road while we talked. Now, we turned back towards the cars. I had an idea.

'We'll put the stuff in my car. Drive up together. Leave the Lincoln here. After it gets dark, you can bring it up close to the house. No lights. Bring it in as close as you can, and keep it out of sight.'

He shrugged, looking puzzled.

'If you say so. But what's the idea?'

'I don't really know myself. But if we have a second car, that's something we know, but nobody else does. It could just give us an edge, if we need one.'

We tossed his stuff into the Chev, and drove up to Rivers Bend. It still wasn't quite dark, but already a few lights had been switched on. The air was heavy after the heat of the day, with a feel to it that said tomorrow would be as hot again.

Kathryn Nolan was sitting on one of the white-painted chairs on the verandah. She'd changed out of her working clothes and into an emerald green number that shimmered in the dying rays of the sun. Thompson cleared his throat appreciatively. I could see what he meant.

'Ah, Mr Preston. I'd almost given you up.'

Her voice was somehow lacking in the warmth I like to hear from attractive women.

'Given me up?' I repeated needlessly.

'Yes. Mr Rivers told me to wait until you arrived, before I went home.'

'I'm sorry if I've kept you. I had no idea.'

She smiled then, and some of the frost dissipated.

'Don't mind me. I'm just grouchy because I'm keeping some people waiting. Now, there's food in the kitchen, if you're hungry. Pedro and Anna have already gone home, I'm afraid.'

She didn't say it's all right for some people, but that was what she meant.

'So who will be here tonight?' I queried. 'I mean, staying all night.'

'All the family, I imagine. Larry's out at the moment, but he said nothing about staying out all night.'

'Does he do that sometimes?'

Miss Nolan looked at me steadily.

'I wouldn't know. I'm a private

secretary, Mr Preston. It's no part of my job to keep tabs on family movements.'

'No, of course it isn't. And Lynda Lee, is she around?'

'She's off out at one of the neighbours' houses. Some other young people are having a party. And your guess is as good as mine as to what time that will finish.'

'Right. So it's just Mr Rivers and us. Oh, I ought to have introduced my partner, Sam Thompson. Kathryn Nolan.'

Sam mumbled something, and she gave him a friendly nod.

'Mr Rivers is working in his study. From what he tells me, he quite often works until midnight and beyond. So it looks as though you and Mr Thompson have the run of the house.'

And don't get it all untidy, her tone clearly implied. She stood up, smoothing at her dress. I could feel what Thompson was thinking. I was thinking the same thing.

'It's a pity you have to rush off,' I told her.

'Yes. But I'll be here in the morning. Around eight-thirty. You wouldn't care to tell me what this is all about?'

'What did Mr Rivers say?' I countered.

'Nothing.'

I grinned an apology.

'Well, he's the boss, I'm afraid. See you in the morning, Kathryn.'

She smiled sweetly.

'Kathryn? No one ever calls me that. To my friends I'm always Kate. You may call me Miss Nolan.'

And that took care of me.

As she walked past Sam, she said 'Goodnight Mr Thomas.'

And that took care of him.

The trim figure disappeared down the steps. Thompson sniffed.

'So much for the big lady-killer,' he scoffed.

'What do you expect, when a girl sees me with a bum like you? There's a thing called guilt by association, you know.'

'There's a thing called the bum's rush too,' he retorted. 'And that is what call-me-Miss Nolan just gave you.'

A car motor sprang to life somewhere out in the dusk. There was a sweep of sudden light and a scrunching of tyres on gravel. Then the sound faded into the distance.

'We'd better get in the house.'

I walked him around, explaining the layout. As we went, we shut all windows, locked all outside doors. Upstairs, I left a couple of lights burning, to give the impression of people up and around. It was quite dark now.

'You'd better come and let Mr Rivers see your face. If he sees a stranger in the middle of the night, he might take a swing at you with a crowbar or something.'

'Right.'

I knocked at the study door, opened it. Rivers was planted firmly behind the desk, watching us approach.

'Thought you ought to see my associate, Sam Thompson, Mr Rivers. It could avoid a misunderstanding during the night.'

Rivers inspected my shambling companion, and nodded.

'Good evening,' he acknowledged. 'I trust you won't be needing me at all.

141

There's really rather a lot of work here to be done.'

He tapped at a pile of papers.

'We'll try not to disturb you,' I promised. Then, pointing at the french doors, I said, 'would you mind locking those when you go to bed? Don't want to make life too easy if anyone pays us a visit.'

Rivers nodded seriously.

'Of course. I will see to it. Goodnight.'

And we found ourselves back outside the room.

'Friendly, ain't he?'

'We're not exactly house guests,' I reminded. 'What do you expect? We're here to do a job, and that's all.'

'I wouldn't mind starting work in the kitchen. Some of that grub looked pretty good.'

'You go ahead. There's nothing more we can do now, but wait. I'll sack out in the living room for an hour or two. Give me a call at two a.m.'

He disappeared towards the kitchen. I humped my blankets into the comfort of the big room and dropped them in a corner. It was too hot for any covering. Pulling an ottoman to where I could see into the paved area behind the house, I stretched out, using cushions as pillows.

Some people can sleep anywhere. I'm one of them.

9

A travesty of Judith Harvey Rivers' face leered obscenely from the nine foot canvas. In front of it, a man in a white coat ran up and down dabbing feverishly with a twelve-inch brush. Blood dripped from one corner of her mouth, blood from living flesh clutched in her outstretched hand. Rivers shouted hoarsely 'No, no, it isn't neat enough, it has to be neat.' Another man shouted back 'You want it neat? How's this?' A ragged tear appeared in the canvas, and a body was propelled through. A bloated, putrescent thing that might once have been a woman. The frantic painter turned, and it wasn't a brush in his hand at all. It was a giant syringe. He had no face, only strips of blackened skin draped over a skull, grinning in evil anticipation as the needle jabbed towards my frozen eyes.

'Hey.'

Suddenly, I had the use of my arms,

and I flailed out at him.

'Crissakes, Preston.'

My gaze focussed blearily. Three feet away, Larry Rivers sat on the floor, rubbing at a shoulder.

'Huh?'

They'd all gone. All the others. The boy scrambled to his feet, using language he had no right to know. I swung my feet down to the floor, rubbing at my eyes. According to my watch it was one-twenty in the a.m.

'What happened?'

I had a pretty good idea what had happened, but I was stalling for time to get myself awake.

'What happened was you,' he said nastily. 'Do you always slug everybody who wakes you up?'

'Did I do that? I'm sorry. I mean it. But there was this terrible dream, and somebody was going to kill me.'

His handsome face was still angry.

'Just keep up your little habits,' he suggested, 'and you'll have no trouble finding volunteers.'

'I told you I was sorry,' I said shortly. 'I

don't intend to open a vein. What did you want, anyway?'

'Study door. It's locked. I'm worried about the old man.'

His voice was still resentful, but I could detect his concern.

'Locked? Well, he probably doesn't want people prowling around in there.'

Larry shook his head impatiently.

'You don't understand. He hasn't gone to bed. He has to be in that study. And he doesn't answer.'

That cleared away the last of the fog.

'Where's Thompson?'

'Who?'

'Thompson. The man who's working with me.'

His eyes were blank.

'I don't know about any man. Nobody around when I came home. Well, what about it?'

I got up, fully awake at last.

'Let's go.'

The hallway outside the study was in darkness. I snapped at the switch. Nothing. The door wouldn't open. I banged on it.

'Mr Rivers. Open up. It's me, Preston.'
Silence.

'Is there another key?' I demanded.

'None that I know of. We'd better break it down.'

'Break it down?' I said scornfully. 'You watch too many cops and robbers. This isn't some cheap tenement. That door is solid wood and so is the surround. Try charging that, the only thing you'll break is your shoulder.'

'You already did that,' he snapped. 'So what's the answer?'

There was only one that I knew. If I was acting too hastily, Bernard L. Rivers would have quite a bit to say. But I hadn't time to argue with myself.

'Stand to one side,' I ordered.

Larry's mouth didn't quite drop open as I produced the thirty-eight. Thumbing back the safety, I pointed it at the lock. The gun sounded like a cannon in the confined hall. This time, the gold handle turned downwards, and I went in with a rush. Such a rush, I almost trod on Rivers' head. He was lying on the floor, hand stretched out towards the door. All the lights were on.

Kneeling beside the body, I felt for his heart. A faint beating said he wasn't dead. Not yet. There was no blood on his back. I heaved him over, looking for frontal wounds. I didn't understand it.

'Is he dead?'

Larry's voice was anxious beside me. Whether anxious that his father should be dead, or anxious that he shouldn't, I had no way of telling.

'No,' I said shortly. 'Does he have a heart condition?'

'Not that I know of.'

'We need a doctor here. You know who to call?'

'Yup.'

'Call him. Never mind what time it is. You tell him this is life and death.'

The young man knew it was no time for arguments. He went to the gold desk-instrument and picked it up. I stood, staring down at the man on the carpet. No blood, no sign of any wounds. No facial discolouration to suggest any form of convulsion. While Larry stood, waiting for someone to pick up the receiver at the other end, I prowled around, feeling helpless. I tried the french doors, but they were locked. But someone else had been here. Someone who locked the study door from outside. Who? And where was Thompson? Then my eyes lighted on the water-jug. Knowing it was almost certainly a waste of time, I poured some water and sniffed at it. Nothing. I put down the glass. Then I changed my mind, picked it up again, and took a sip. Not swallowing any, I sluiced the water from side to side in my mouth. I was about to give up, and feeling rather foolish, when the inside of one cheek began to burn. Then the other. I spat out the liquid. Larry had started talking to somebody at the other end. He looked astonished when I spat, more so when I grabbed the receiver from him.

'Doctor, it's poison. No taste, no smell. What do I do? Who am I? what in hell does it matter who I am? My name is Preston, and your patient could be dying here. What do I do? — In the water jug —Yes, I did. It burned my cheeks — O.K. Do I call an ambulance or what? You'll be here — Yeah — Yeah. Don't waste any time, doctor. There's no one here qualified to deal with this.'

I slammed down the phone.

'Larry, your father has been poisoned. The doctor will be at least twenty minutes getting here. That leaves you and me. We have to get him on his feet, make him sick, and walk him around. Understand?'

He was all attention. I'd been afraid he might go to pieces.

'Got it. How do we make him throw up?'

'Mustard. Let's find that first.'

We were busy then, too busy to think much beyond the next immediate physical task. Anybody who hasn't had any need to lift a six feet four inches man from a prone position, when he's unconscious, and all dead weight, is missing a new experience. It was messy, too.

After we succeeded in making him ill, we set about half-dragging, half-carrying him out of the house, and into the night air. His breathing was very low.

'Walk,' I shouted at him. 'You lazy

bastard, Rivers. Walk.'

I'd read somewhere that a mixture of angry authority and insult was a good way to penetrate the unconscious mind. And I didn't spare Rivers in either department. Larry, after one shocked look in my direction, seemed intuitively to latch on to what I was trying to do. He even began to join in, particularly with the insults. Some of the stuff he produced made me wonder whether he did some of his drinking with drill sergeants from the marine corps base.

It began to work. First Rivers tried to move a leg, then the other. I sneered at his efforts. Loudly. Loudly enough to offend his inner manliness, force him to some kind of response.

'It's working.'

There was no hiding the relief in his son's voice. I winked at him. He was no more relieved than me.

'He only just started,' I replied. 'Keep him going.'

We were still at it when yellow headlamps flared across the grass, lighting up what would have been a strange scene if the doctor hadn't been expecting it. Door slamming, and feet hurrying towards us.

'Good work,' snapped a crisp voice. 'Just hold him still, while I give him a shot.'

The doctor kneeled down, opening his black bag, rooting around inside. I watched him tear back Rivers' short sleeve, and insert the thin needle.

'You must be Mr Preston. My name is Hoskins.'

The voice was clipped New England. I took my first look at the horse-playing psychiatrist. He was of medium height, with dark curly hair above a good-natured, but at that moment worried-looking face.

'How do,' I replied.

'Good thing you were here,' he muttered, working away. 'Oh, no offense to you Larry. What I mean is, this is a two-man job. You could never have lifted your father by yourself.'

'I know what you meant.'

Larry's voice was cool. He didn't like Dr Hoskins. I wondered whether it meant anything, decided I was always looking for sinister motives. There's nothing in the constitution that says everybody has to love everybody else.

After that, we were just hospital orderlies. We did whatever Hoskins told us for the next half-hour or so. Then, by this time with a lot more cooperation from the patient himself, we finally had Rivers in his bed.

'I'll be around downstairs if you need me, doctor.'

He mumbled something, without looking round.

'I guess I'll hang around here for a while,' Larry said.

I nodded, and went out of the bedroom. In all the excitement, and with the top priority being the need to keep Rivers alive, I hadn't been able to look for Sam Thompson. At first I'd thought he'd fallen asleep on the job, but when he didn't show after all the noise that had been made, I was thinking a lot different.

First of all, I searched the house. I didn't find Thompson, but I found something else. The light from the study spilled out into the darkened hall, shining on something bright. It was the key to the door. Whoever locked it had simply dropped the key there. Maybe they'd been disturbed by Larry's arrival. Or maybe Larry himself — no. No, that would make no sense. The intention had been to prevent Rivers getting out of the study for help. For Larry to have done that, only to come and wake me immediately, would be to spoil his own intentions.

There was no sign of Sam anywhere close to the house. It was getting to be a big mystery. Until I remembered the Lincoln. He could have walked down to the car, decided to take a short nap in the comfort of the driving seat. That would explain why all the commotion at the house hadn't disturbed him. Nobody's temper is very good at two-thirty in the morning, and mine is no exception. By the time I'd made the journey to the parked car, I was in no mood for excuses.

Thompson didn't offer one. He was lying face down on the grass beside the road. The way his great frame was spread-eagled showed he hadn't adopted the position for comfort. I felt at the back of his head, and found a bruise the size of an egg. It took a couple of minutes to rouse him.

'How'd it happen, Sam?'

He sat upright, cursing with an admirable fluency. Overhead, the pale moonlight filtered through wispy drifting cloud, creating ground shadows that landed, shifted, disappeared. Now you see it, now you don't. Every rock, every bush, became an object of suspicion, a place of concealment for unidentified evil. I kept moving my glance around against surprise. From what?

'Sam.'

'I hear you,' he grumbled. 'My head.'

'Did you see who it was?'

'No. They could of been hiding behind the car. I just don't know. One minute I'm unlocking the door, the next thing I know is the beautiful music.'

'You O.K. to walk?'

I'd already done my share of carrying people around for that night. After he'd climbed unsteadily to his feet, I told him about the attempt on Rivers.

'Poison?' he echoed. 'It won't go together. Know what I mean? We're all set to meet this frontal assault with the Molotov cocktails. That's an outside thing, trying to get in. But poison? Water jugs? That's inside already. They don't fit right.'

That was already nagging at my mind too. We walked back to the house in silence. Sam had a sore head to think about, and there was plenty else for me to think about. When we marched through the open front door, Hoskins was coming downstairs, talking quietly to Larry.

'How's the patient?' I greeted.

'He's asleep now. You two probably saved his life.'

'Got another one for you, Doctor,' I told him. 'My friend here has been slugged.'

To do him justice the little medic didn't argue. He walked up to Thompson, and around behind him, probing gently.

'Yuck,' said Sam. At least that's what it sounded like.

'H'm. A nasty bump. Somebody hit

you pretty hard, Mr — ?'

'Thompson. Sam Thompson.'

'Mr Thompson.' Hoskins rooted around in his bag again. 'Wet this piece of lint, pour some of this on it' — 'this' was a small bottle — 'and dab it over the area. It won't do much good, but at least you can say you received medical attention.'

Sam grinned ruefully, and shambled away to do as he was told. Hoskins turned to Larry.

'I wonder if there's any chance of some coffee?'

Larry was evidently glad of the chance to do something useful.

'Sure. I'll rustle some up. Mr Preston?'

Now I was Mr Preston.

'Fine, yeah,' I nodded.

'Let's go into the study.'

I walked along beside the doctor, busy with my own thoughts. Not the least of them was what explanation Larry might have given for my being there at all. I knew a great deal about Dr Franklyn Hoskins. How much did he know about me?

Inside the study, he put the all-purpose

bag down on the desk, and parked in one of the chairs. I did the same. He studied me with professional eyes.

'Well now, Mr Preston, you and I are going to have to talk to each other, it seems.'

While you're waiting to find out what kind of cards the other guy is holding, it's always useful to make a small production out of locating your cigarettes, selecting one, and making smoke.

'Go ahead, doc. I'm listening.'

'Very well.' He placed his fingertips together, drumming lightly. 'First of all, there's the legal position here. Mr Rivers is my patient, and I have a duty to him. That is first and foremost. I have discharged that duty. I am satisfied that I have done all I can, in the medical sense. But I also have a duty to the community.'

He seemed to expect some contribution, but I hadn't heard enough yet.

'Community?' I repeated, looking blank.

'Certainly, the community,' he snapped. 'I'm certain you know as well as I do that the law had been broken here tonight. A direct contravention of the

state penal code. Whatever other free-
doms we may enjoy, we are not permitted
to commit suicide.'

The blankness on my face was now
real.

'Suicide?'

10

I seemed to be taxing the man's patience. He clucked with annoyance, and shifted around in his chair.

'It's fairly obvious, isn't it? He was alone in here, it was the early hours of the morning. Nobody forced him to take that poison, whatever it was. A man, alone in his study, the small hours. The circumstances are classic. If you hadn't been as resourceful as you were, he would have been successful. Whether he will thank you remains to be seen. The point at issue is, am I to report this or not? Barney Rivers is by way of being a friend of mine.'

Barney, I reflected. A man who would have to be very close to the Bernard L. Rivers I knew before he started calling him Barney. I was going to have to talk to this man. Carefully.

'Doctor, I don't think you have all the facts,' I began.

'I think I do,' he interrupted. 'All the relevant facts, anyway. Barney's son told me in detail what happened here.'

That made it clearer. Larry had no way of knowing about the key.

'He didn't have all the facts,' I assured the listening man. 'He assumed, the same way I did, that the door was locked on the inside. When we discovered his father lying there, it was not time to be checking on details.'

'And?' He leaned forward with interest.

'When I was looking for my partner, Thompson, after we got Mr Rivers upstairs, I found the doorkey.' I pointed out through the open door. 'It was lying out there in the hall. That door was locked from outside, Doctor.'

The bewilderment on his face was plain.

'But that would mean — '

'Oh, yes. It would mean that you and I have to talk, just as you said. But not about suicide, Doctor. What we have here is a case of attempted murder.'

'My God.'

Reaching over, he pulled down his bag

and rummaged inside. When his hand came out, he was holding a small bottle.

'Brandy,' he announced. 'I carry it for fainting cases. And the occasional attempted murder. Join me?'

'Why not?'

The brandy was a smooth round warmth inside me. The doctor was quickly onto his second shot, with no more than a half-hearted offer to me this time. I refused.

'I don't understand it,' he muttered. 'I mean, the man is no saint. Anybody might lose their temper with him, just like any other man. A gun, a knife, perhaps. But poison?'

He seemed to be hoping I could offer some kind of explanation, but I hadn't any. It was a good opportunity to get him talking on his own subject. Always a good way to calm people down.

'You said just now 'whatever it was',' I reminded. 'You were speaking of the poison. What did you mean by that?'

'It means I don't know what it was. Odourless, colourless, practically tasteless until it's too late. You established that

162

much. Could be one of a number of things. I'll analyse a sample of the jug contents. It should be relatively easy to establish. Why do you ask?'

'Once we know what it is, it'll help towards identifying whoever put it there.'

As an explanation, it seemed enough to me. Not to him.

'How will it do that?'

I squinted at him to be sure he wasn't kidding me. I don't kid too well at that time of the morning.

'Access,' I replied. 'Being a doctor, you've been around poisons so long they're just part of life's background. To the rest of us, poison is a naughty word. Stuff to keep on the top shelf so the kids don't drink it by mistake. And the kind of thing we can buy is always strongly coloured and clearly identified. If I walked into a pharmacist and asked for a nice lethal dose of something with no colour or smell, to help my poor aunt with her bad chest, he'd send for the man with the nightstick.'

He nodded, still not convinced.

'Yes, yes, I see that. But there are plenty

of people who work with poisons around them. Part of the environment. Paint shops, many places.'

'Right,' I confirmed. 'You take my point exactly. Once you identify it as Formula YZ or whatever, we'll know the type of place it's to be found. The number of people who could reach that water jug is small. The connection might be obvious.'

'Ah,' he beamed. 'Yes. Exactly so. You're an interesting man, Mr Preston. First of all, you were here in the house in the small hours. Then you just happened to be carrying a weapon with enough power to blow a lock off a door. Then you kept your head in dealing with Rivers, to the possible extent that he kept his life as a result. Now you deliver your standard introductory lecture in the use of poisons in the area of homicide. Forgive me if I sound inquisitive but you don't seem to fit the standard pattern of passer-by.'

'You mean who the hell am I?'

He made a deprecatory face and poured himself the last of the brandy. Then he waited.

'I'm a security man. Here to advise Mr

Rivers about making this place a little safer.'

'Ah. Well in a way, I suppose that gives you some kind of official status. But it doesn't help with my problem about reporting what happened here.'

'Why not leave it till the morning?' I suggested. 'After all, there's really only family people involved. Or so it seems. Victim or no, Mr Rivers may have quite a bit to say if he wakes up to find his family being given the third degree all over the house.'

He considered this, over a near-empty glass.

'More or less what I was thinking,' he agreed. 'There's Larry, Lynda Lee — where is she, by the way?'

'Party,' I supplied. 'They'll probably bring home the remains any time now.'

'That girl needs — well, never mind. So there are these two, then Pedro and Anna, can't rule them out. There's Miss Dolan, the secretary.'

'Nolan,' I corrected.

'Nolan, is it? All right. We'd have to find out if there were any visitors of course. That about sums it up.'

'You'll never make cop, Doctor.'

'Huh?'

I pointed at my manly chest.

'There's me.'

'You. Well, yes, I guess so. Technically, yes.'

'And Livvy,' I shot out suddenly.

He froze in the chair for tenth part of a second. It was enough for me. Then he said enquiringly

'Livvy?'

'You can't have forgotten old Livvy so soon?' I jeered. 'Olivia Jayne Hart. You've been keeping her locked up these past two years. She only broke out a couple of days ago. You're going to have to watch that memory.'

The glass made a small rattling sound as he set it down on the desk.

'It seems I shall have to ask you again, Mr Preston. Just who are you?'

'I told you. My job here is security. Livvy says she's going to burn the house down. Mr Rivers doesn't think she should. I'm to try stopping her.'

'I see.' He fingered at his loose-knotted

tie. 'I don't know what Barney Rivers told you about this young woman, but I must tell you we're dealing with a very disturbed personality. Severely disordered. Not responsible. In any case, she can have nothing to do with this poison affair.'

'I'm inclined to agree with you,' I replied. 'But we can't leave her out. Not when we talk to the police.'

He stood up abruptly, went to a cupboard on the far side of the room, and opened the door. Light streamed dully from an impressive array of bottles. Lifting one out, he brought it back to his chair and poured himself four fingers of what looked like scotch. Nobody asked me to the party. Now he lifted the glass to his lips, and poured the stuff away like water. He stood quite still for a few moments, then shook his head as a violent tremor went through him, starting with his face, and working down. Then he gave a deep sigh, a long, relieved expelling of breath. The man who now resumed his seat opposite me was a confident, smiling man with bright alert eyes.

'Yes, yes, the police of course. Well you know, there would be nothing to gain on anyone's part, by involving Olivia in any of this. I'm sure Mr Rivers will agree. He wouldn't want you to start the authorities chasing that poor girl. Why don't we just wait until we can talk to him?'

And it was settled. Just like that. Or so he thought. I chuckled.

'You're quite a character,' I told him. 'You really think it's that simple, don't you? You think all we do is hand over the problem to Rivers. After all, it's his show, he's the producer. And the moneyman. He hands each of us our parts. You will say this, I will say that. I mean you really seem to think that's the way it's gonna be, don't you?'

'Not the way you put it. Of course not. But you have to have regard to Mr Rivers' wishes.'

He still didn't get what I was driving at.

'I don't lie to any cops. Not for you, not for Rivers, nobody. If the cops are in it, then they're in it all the way. You had better adjust all your thinking around that one fact, Doctor. Unless, of course — '

I paused for effect. It had an effect.

'Well go on,' he prompted eagerly. 'Unless what?'

'Unless it's decided they are best left out of it altogether,' I finished.

That had him guessing.

'You seem to be a man of mixed views,' he said tetchily. 'One minute you insist on telling the police everything, the next nothing at all. Perhaps you would explain a little further.'

To me it was all quite clear. So, I explained anyway.

'You're not paying attention. I said, once the police are brought in, I have no intention of misleading them. But it's no part of my wishes to go running to them voluntarily. In is all the way in. Out is completely out. Does that make it clearer?'

'Not much, but it'll have to do for now. Then I take it we do nothing further in that respect until the morning?'

'Unless you'd like to tell me a whole lot more about Miss Hart,' I suggested. Without conviction.

His smile was less than warm.

'I have every intention of telling you precisely nothing, until Mr Rivers is party to the conversation. In fact, I'm going to get some sleep during what remains of the night. I suggest you do the same.'

'Will you go home?' I asked.

'Not worth it. I'll stretch out in a chair in Barney's room. He might need something. One can never be sure.'

He walked out and left me sitting there. I heard voices outside in the hall, then Sam Thompson shuffled in.

'How's the head?'

'Just like any head that's been run over by a train. Terrible.'

Sam is very predictable. The time he starts complaining is the time you know everything is going to be O.K. My watch indicated a couple of minutes short of four a.m.

'It's four o'clock,' I pointed out. 'Think you can see the night through? I ought to catch some shuteye. Lot to do tomorrow. You can sleep all day, if you want.'

'I guess so,' he said grudgingly. 'Bumps cost extra, by the way. Did I mention that?'

'Don't be such a softie. You'll live. Don't go too far away from this room, Sam. Could just be some finger prints on that jug.'

I left him sprawled out, still dabbing at the lump on his head. As I was passing the fireplace, I glanced up at the black velvet curtains. Maybe I could talk Rivers into letting me have one more glimpse of Judith's picture before the job was finished.

Outside the house, there was a sudden squeal of brakes, followed by the sound of impacting metal and breaking glass. I made the door in three strides and ducked through onto the verandah, the .38 hard and comforting in my hand.

'Ooh, it's Dick Tracy. Hallo Dick Tracy. Are you going to rescue poor little me?'

A small powerful sports-car was scrunched against the bottom steps of the stone staircase. Lynda Lee Rivers leaned against the car, moonlight striking against the golden hair tumbled around her face. She was wearing a shiny red dress with no top, no back and not much of anything else. Now she waved a gold evening purse at me reproachfully.

'You didn't even ask if I was hurt.'

I felt foolish, and the gun was suddenly an obtrusion. I shoved it away, and glowered at her.

'Are you hurt?'

'Huh.'

She swung the driving door shut with a bang. A jagged lump of glass slipped from a shattered headlamp, and fragmented on the stonework. Lynda Lee pulled herself carefully erect, and began her uncertain ascent of the steps. Her face was haughty, with the carefully aloof mask of the slightly stoned.

'Fat lot you care, Mr Tracy.'

'Preston,' I corrected.

When she was level with me she paused, inspecting me with great care. She even ran a finger down the side of my face.

'Preston, eh? You're kind of cute.'

'You're kind of drunk,' I told her brutally. 'Go to bed.'

'M'm, lovely. Are you coming?'

'After I feed the pigs. Go on to bed.'

She took a step back, still studying me.

172

Then she did a pirouette. Or something that started out that way. She finished the movement facing away from me, and had to make focussing motions to get me lined up again.

'I'm only eighteen, you know,' she confided. 'Some people think I look older. A whole lot older. What do you think?'

'I think you're seventeen, and you behave like a spoiled child of ten. Go away.'

She stamped her foot, causing her body to shake. I could see why some people might have taken her for older. I wondered where she'd been all night, who she'd been with. Whether they had assumed she was a lot older, and treated her that way. Well, it wasn't my problem.

I made a threatening move towards her, and she jumped back with a small gasp.

'O.K. I'm going, I'm going.'

She went into the house, negotiating the doorway at the second attempt. I went to inspect the damage on the car. There was nothing wrong that two days work and several hundred dollars wouldn't put right. The moonlight was too weak to show up the name on the registration. I snapped my lighter and read 'N. Bravington'. So the bullion-king's daughter was playing games with friend Nigel. I didn't like it. I also didn't like the way he left her to drive home by herself, with all that booze inside her. Serve him right that she'd smashed up his car. He could count himself lucky she hadn't smashed herself up along with it.

Thompson stood outside the house waiting for me.

'Thought you might need some help,' he told me.

'Just Cinderella trying to get home before sunrise,' I explained.

'Uh, Uh.' He nodded. 'That's Dracula, you're thinking of. Cinderella does an earlier shift. Anyway, she made one helluva mess of the coach. Is she O.K?'

'I think so. She's gone to bed. I'll see you later, Sam.'

I left him contemplating the damage, and went into the darkness of the living room. Might as well catch whatever was left of the night. Kicking off my shoes, I

174

lay down on the ottoman, feeling for my cushions.

Instead I found flesh. Warm, living flesh, over me, all around me, writhing and pressing. Lynda Lee Rivers was as naked as the day she was born, but she'd grown a lot since. I tried to push her away, but the trouble was wherever I put my hands there was more of her. Her own hands were everywhere, probing and pulling me to her. Red lips were clamped firmly over mine, and her legs had mine trapped.

Wrenching my mouth free I whispered urgently

'Honey, honey, listen.'

The writhing stopped for a moment.

'Honey?' she repeated. 'Well, it's a start.'

To leave my mouth free she started chewing my ear. I stroked along her spine as evidence of my intentions.

'This is too crowded, this thing we're on. I'm no good inside the house, anyway,' I muttered urgently. 'I'm a grass man.'

She placed her hands either side of my

head, and levered herself up, just enough to stare into my face. Her eyes were dancing.

'Grass? You have to have grass? Well, what are we doing here?'

We stood up together, and she pressed herself against me in a long embrace. I was getting to enjoy it. That meant it was time to move. I scooped her up in my arms, and she giggled joyfully, clasping her arms around my neck.

'A grass man,' she repeated in my ear. 'Imagine. This is going to be something else.'

'After tonight,' I assured her, making my voice thick, 'you'll never walk past grass and feel the same way.'

I picked over the paving stones to the lawn.

'This'll do. Right here,' she said urgently.

'No. I have my eye on the exact spot. Kiss me, and close your eyes.'

She did that and I joined in, with mixed enjoyment and regret. A few more paces and I lifted my head away.

'This is it lover. We've arrived.'

I didn't have to throw her very far. Just a few feet to ensure she was clear of the climbing ladder. She hit the swimming pool like a tidal wave, a sudden scream of rage ending in a flurry of bubbles and choking.

'You lousy bastard,' she spluttered, treading water, 'I'll — '

Leaning over, I pushed her head under again. When I let her up, she was gasping for breath.

'When I get out of here — '

I gave her another ducking. This time she was scarcely able to speak. She tried to swing a fist at me, but the blow wouldn't have killed a moth.

'Last time,' I assured her. 'We've got to stop meeting like this.'

This time when she came up, she was too spent for rage. Instead there were tears. Little girl tears.

'Now you're going to towel off, and get to bed like a good little girl, and nobody hears another peep out of you tonight. Is that right?'

She nodded, sniffling. I picked her up one of the huge beach towels from a chair and held it out for her to climb into. Wordlessly, she wrapped it around herself and walked away into the house.

I went back to the ottoman. The only flesh on it was mine. It seemed less friendly, somehow.

11

Something tickled my ear. I brushed at it with feeble, ineffective fingers. It tickled again.

'Coffee.'

I cracked one eyelid. Searing sunlight rushed in, attacking my pupil. I tried again, making a shade with my hand.

Lynda Lee sat a few feet away, watching me. Today she wasn't Irma any more. Today, we auditioned for Rebecca of Sunnybrook Farm. The gleaming honey hair was brushed straight back, and caught in a ponytail. Her pretty face was all the prettier for being scrubbed shining clean. She wore a severely-tailored white blouse, tucked into faded jeans. No shoes. I knew she'd had the same amount of sleep as me, but she looked like an ad for the health farm. Nobody needed to tell me what I looked like.

Steam rose from the cup in her waiting hand.

'Coffee,' she repeated.

I swung into some semblance of an upright position.

'What time is it?'

'Drink this, and I'll tell you.'

I reached out, burned my fingers, grumbled, found the handle, lifted the drink to my mouth. It was strong and hot.

'Good.'

I looked at my watch, wondering why I hadn't done that in the first place. It was seven twenty.

'About last night,' she said, 'I want to thank you.'

Nobody can look totally innocent at that hour of the day. I did the best I could.

'Why? What happened last night?' I countered.

Soft green eyes held mine in a level gaze.

'You know perfectly well what happened. I came on like the third whore on the left in some Roman orgy. You decided not to play. Thank you, Mark.'

Mark, I wondered? Thinking back to

our conversation earlier, I couldn't recall telling her that.

'Mark?' I challenged. 'Where did you get that?'

'Mr Thompson told me. We've been talking in the kitchen. He's nice.'

Petulantly, I queried.

'So how come he's Mr Thompson, and I'm Mark? What's wrong with Mr Preston?'

'Nothing that I can see. I'd say you were O.K. plus. But after all, we have been in bed together, and midnight bathing and all. I would say 'Mr' would be kind of formal, having regard to all the circumstances. Don't you agree?'

The grin was infectious, even at that hour. I chuckled, rooting around for cigarettes. The pack had fallen on the floor. I pulled the harsh smoke down gratefully, and looked a long time at this pretty thing, trying to connect her with the previous night.

'Do you always carry on that way?'

Her eyes dropped, and a slight blush tinged her upper cheeks. Last night she'd only been dangerous. This way she was dynamite.

'No, I don't.' The voice was small. 'As a matter of fact, if you'd had a different reaction, you'd have been in for a surprise. You see, I haven't — that is to say, I don't — '

'It's all right. You needn't go on,' I told her gently. 'This time it happened to be me. Next time it won't be. Learn something.'

'Yes. I don't know what came over me. I don't usually drink, you see, just a glass of wine now and then. Maybe that was it. It would have to be, wouldn't you think?'

Enough with the true confessions, I decided. Putting the empty cup down on the floor, I asked.

'What's with you and Bravington?'

That brought her back to the present.

'Who told you about him?' she demanded.

I jerked a vague thumb towards the outside world.

'Recognised the car,' I lied.

'Cripes, yes. What'll I do if my father recognises it? He can't stand Nigel.'

'Oh? Why's that? Did they have a fight?'

Her tone was bitter when she replied.

'My father can't stand anybody who shows any interest in his pure, lilywhite daughter. Thinks all they want is his money. Him and that damned money.'

'He wants to get those money bags out of his eyes, and take a square look at you. Money is not what springs to mind.'

Her face softened again.

'You're nice. But that's how he is. And he hates Nigel more than the rest of them.'

'You still didn't tell me why.'

'Because of Judith. She was my father's second wife. Or perhaps you knew that?'

'Yes, I've heard about her.'

Judith. My mind was fully awake now. This girl could put flesh on that picture out in the hall. She'd seen her walk, heard her laugh. Talked with her. Keeping my voice casual, I asked:

'What was she like?'

'Judith? Oh, she was gorgeous. I never really knew my mother you know. She died in an accident when I was a baby. A fire.'

'Yes, I know. A terrible thing to have happened.'

Lynda Lee nodded.

'As you say. But most people don't seem to understand that if you've never known your own mother, you can't feel the same sense of loss. Does that sound terrible?'

I thought before replying.

'No, I don't think so. I think I can understand that. And I think you're telling me that you didn't resent Judith coming here to take her place.'

'Oh, you do understand,' she exclaimed. 'Only I sometimes feel somehow disloyal about that. No, I didn't resent her. Quite the reverse. All I could think was there was going to be a woman about the house, someone I could talk to, confide in. And she was everything a girl could have hoped for.'

Or a man, I thought. Especially a man.

'I'd like to hear about her.'

I didn't tell the girl how much.

'Judith? She was warm. Full of vitality, lots of fun, interested in everything, a good friend. She could be all kinds of people. The grand actress was one. Judith could dominate a dinner party when she wanted. Have all the men running around to light cigarettes, get her a cushion. And all with a kind of wink behind it. It was all a big act for the poor little males. Even the other women didn't mind too much. Another time she'd be the lady of the house. Didn't care what she did. Dust, polish, cook, anything. She used to say a woman who doesn't know how to make a home is only half a woman. Made me do it, too. I'd always been useless around the house. But the example was there. If a woman who looked like Judith could roll up her sleeves, so could I.'

She paused, probably for breath.

'It was good coffee. Mostly it's just a black drink,' I said.

The pony tail jumped as she wagged her head.

'You just have to take a little extra trouble. No magic involved. Judith taught me how. You ought to try one of my souffles sometime.'

'I'll look forward to it. She must have been quite a girl. What on earth do you suppose happened? I mean, her taking off in the boat that way. Was she an impulsive person?'

'I guess she was, sometimes. Outdoors, she was great. Sail, swim, ride, she'd try anything.'

'Ride?' I queried.

'We had a few horses then. This is great country for riding, you know. After she — after what happened, my father got rid of them. He got rid of many things that reminded him of her.'

'Understandable. But if he didn't want to be reminded, why did he keep the picture? I mean, the way he has it, in that dominating position, it reminds everybody all the time.'

She held her feet out in front of her, inspecting the toes.

'You have to know him to understand that. It puzzled me for a long time, until I worked it out. It didn't seem to make any sense. He made such an act of getting rid of her clothes, her jewellery. Even a stray handkerchief would upset him. And yet, as you say, the portrait. How well do you know him?'

'Not well at all. I just met him today. That is, yesterday.'

The pony-tail bounced again.

'He's a very methodical person. Very detached sometimes. He can't stand things which aren't in neat, orderly lines. House things, business things. And people things.'

'That can't be too easy to live with,' I suggested.

'Live with?' she snorted. 'You really don't know him. Nobody lives with him. You live around him, close by him. In the vicinity, you might say. But not with him.'

It was a sore subject. But I wasn't about to leave it.

'Yet Judith managed it.'

'I suppose. I wasn't really old enough to observe them as a man/woman relationship. Too busy growing up, and being absorbed in my own life.'

'You still didn't give me your theory about why he kept the picture,' I pressed. 'You left him being methodical.'

'Oh. Well, all I can say is how I figured it. The picture only reminds him when he wants to be reminded. Most of the time it's just a pair of curtains on a wall. Nobody else knows how that control panel of his works. And so there is no possibility of him suddenly finding her there. When he decides it's time to be reminded, and only then, he'll stand there making like a space engineer, and look at her. Then she goes back behind the shutters. It's just like some external corner of his mind, to be opened for inspection as required.'

Remote. Detached. And cold, too.

'That is one creepy theory,' I told her.

'It isn't only mine,' she replied defensively. 'Larry agrees with me. We sort of worked it out between us.'

'Larry agrees with you about what?'

We both turned towards the doorway. Larry stood there, scratching at untidy hair, and looking about as fresh and bubbly as a three-day old fried egg. It was my guess he'd stayed awake, watching out for his father. His cold, remote father.

'What's all this stuff I agree with?' he repeated.

Lynda Lee repeated what she'd been

saying about the picture in the hall. He listened to her, but he was watching me.

When she had finished speaking, he said carelessly

'Oh, that. You ought to know that baby sister and I don't agree too often, so make notes when we do. She's right about the lonely old miser, and his secret treasure. Did she also tell you he never looks at it when anyone is around? I've only ever seen it twice myself, and I live here. Time was, I would plan how I was going to work out the circuiting on that electronic gear, play games the way the old man does. But I knew I could never do it really. The old gray matter doesn't lean towards the scientific.'

'Huh,' scoffed his sister. 'Why, you even made a production out of changing a burnt-out lamp.'

'I'm the artistic type,' he told her loftily, 'not a mechanic. Was that coffee in that cup?'

'There's some in the kitchen,' I nodded. 'Is your father still asleep?'

'Mm,' he mumbled. 'It's like the action sound from a war movie up there. The old man snoring like a heavy artillery on one side. Doc Hoskins doing the light machine-gun fire on the other.'

'Dr Hoskins?' Lynda Lee's voice was alarmed. 'What's he doing here?'

Larry looked at me. I realised there was no way the girl could have known what had taken place during the night.

'The doctor came over to visit,' I exclaimed. 'Then stayed up so late talking, that he decided to stop over, rather than drive home.'

The young man nodded his approval of my story.

'Guess I'll grab some of that coffee. You want some more?'

He pointed to the empty cup. It was a gesture. We were on the same side.

'Fine.'

When he went out, Lynda Lee shook her head.

'You didn't need to do that, you know.'

'Do what?'

My surprise was not forced.

'Cover up for the doctor that way. He got drunk, didn't he? He wasn't fit to drive his car, so he had to stay here. I'll bet my father was angry.'

'Why should he be angry?'

She shrugged.

'I don't know. None of his business, I would have said. They're quite good friends you know, but they've been quarrelling a lot lately. About the drinking. I've heard my father shouting at him a couple of times.'

'Friends worry about each other,' I reminded. 'What so wrong about that?'

'Oh, nothing. Nothing at all. My father goes on about his duty as a doctor. Responsibility for the lives of others. That kind of thing.'

'Sounds very proper to me.'

We were interrupted by Larry. He came in on the run, and dashed to a radio in the corner, switching it on.

' — have so far been unable to trace the director, Dr Franklyn Hoskins. If the doctor is listening to this news cast, will he please contact the police immediately, at headquarters in Monkton City or any local station.

In a thrilling finale to the State

Championship last evening — '

The set was clicked off. We both looked at Larry Rivers.

'The sanatorium,' he exclaimed. 'It burned down last night.'

12

Lynda gasped.

'Oh, my God. All those people.'

'It's all right, kid. The fire started in some outhouse. They got everybody out in good time. There is one body, so it said on the news, and no one can account for it. Theory is that it was probably some bum who crawled in there for a night's sleep. He could have started the fire with a cigarette.'

He. The boy said he. So it wasn't Olivia Jayne Hart's body they found. She'd threatened Rivers with a fire last night. He'd assumed, as I did, that she meant his own house. Only we'd both been wrong. Now we had a case of arson, and worse. We also had a body, and that made it murder.

Murder means cops. Tough, wide-awake homicide cops. Not the kind of people who are easy to fool. And no people to meet when you're only half-awake. I looked at the two young people.

'I'm going to have to ask you to cooperate,' I told them. 'Don't ask me a lot of questions. Just assume I'm looking out for the family. Larry, go and get your father and Hoskins up out of bed. Don't stand for any arguments. Tell them the police will be here in thirty minutes.'

'Thirty minutes?' he repeated blankly. 'How do you know?'

'Because in fifteen minutes, no more, I'm going to call them.'

He went out on the run.

'Lynda, we'll have the souffles some other time. Right now, what is needed is breakfast. Lots of it. Will you take charge?'

'You got it.' She stood up quickly. 'Why are you calling the police?'

'A man is dead. You heard the radio. Bum or no, he was still a man, and he's dead. The police will want to ask a lot of questions. Dr Hoskins has got to be in shape to deal with them. And your father will want to help all he can. I promise you that.'

She chewed at her lip.

'Yes. Yes, I can see that. I'll get on it.'

Left alone, I walked across to the garden doors, leaning against the frame, and staring out at the day. My mind was a confused jumble of disconnected scraps of information, too unformed and scattered to be called thoughts.

'Sounds like we came to the wrong fire.'

Sam Thompson's voice was an unwelcome intrusion. I really needed these minutes to be by myself.

'Seems so.' My voice was unfriendly.

But Thompson is not too easily put off.

'It also seems we got a whole mess of crime going on around this town, which don't seem to be connected.'

Compelled now to pay attention, I swung round to look at him. He stared back stolidly.

'Go on.'

'Well, here's you and me, standing around in the canyon with our little extinguishers, only nobody needs firemen today. What we get is an attempted murder, and a slug on the head. That is,'

195

he pointed to his skull, 'some of us get slugged on the head. Meantime, back at the sanatorium, is the guy with the matches. You think maybe somebody's been leading us astray, oh captain?'

I snorted irritably.

'I don't know what the hell I think,' I admitted. 'But you're right about one thing. We're certainly at the wrong end of the city.'

'Not necessarily,' he demurred. 'If you hadn't been around to play nursemaid, our employer could well be dead. Then who would pay us?'

Even I could force a small grin at that.

'It has to be cops, Sam.'

'Yeah. I know. The girl just told me. Say, is that really the same one who staggered in here a few hours ago?'

'Same girl,' I confirmed. 'Sort of. But never mind her. We have to talk about what kind of yarn we give to the law.'

Sam had been without sleep too long. His mind was slow.

'Yarn? Why do we need any yarn? We don't burn places down. We don't have any connection. Proving it would take a whole five minutes, with a fair wind. I don't get it.'

I controlled my impatience.

'That is so. But these are policemen, Sam. They're very nosey people. They come out here on a simple job. A routine questioning of Dr Hoskins, who spent the night at a friend's house. And what do they find? They find a couple of characters like us. They'll want to know why. What are we doing here? Did we come out to discuss our latest gold shipment with our fellow-tycoon, Mr Rivers? It seems unlikely.'

'I'm catching you,' he responded. 'We tell 'em we're here to prevent a fire, somebody tried to bump off the tycoon, and the rest of it. They get very interested. You're right, we do need a yarn.'

With some people it takes a little longer. At that moment, Larry came back in, nodded to Sam.

'I've got them both in the library,' he announced. 'Council of war before the police come. Would you mind?'

We followed him out, past Judith's

picture, and although I knew it was hidden securely away, I couldn't resist a sneaking glance, just in case. A smell of frying bacon wafted out from the kitchen direction, and my stomach growled.

In the study, Rivers was back at his old stand, behind the desk. He looked pale, but composed, as he watched us enter. Slumped in a chair to one side was Hoskins. He was a whole lot paler, and far from composed. In fact, he was a mess. Twitching around, jerking his arms, giving his neck odd twists. He looked like any morning in the drunk tank.

'Come in, gentlemen. Now that we're all here, we can discuss the situation before the police are summoned.'

'All here?' I queried. 'What about your daughter?'

'There is no need for her to be involved in any of this,' he told me calmly. 'She would only be upset, and frightened without cause.'

Well, she was his daughter. Maybe he was right.

'How're you feeling, Mr Rivers?'

He rested his forearms on the table in

front of him, and looked at me over clenched hands.

'Rather shaky, but otherwise very well. I'm told you saved my life last night, Mr Preston. It sounds ridiculously inadequate to thank you, but those are the only words I have.'

I mumbled something about doing what I could.

'And a good thing for me you were here to do it. It was a very stupid mistake for me to make, and I'm lucky to be alive.'

'Mistake?' I knew how foolish it sounded.

'Yes. I always clean the gold items in this room personally. It's a special job. If you leave it to other people, they just rub away at the surface, and in a few years your gold is half-thickness. So I do it myself. Somehow, a little of the special fluid I use got into the water I was drinking. I offer no excuse for sheer stupidity. If Larry hadn't become suspicious, and you hadn't done what you did, I should have paid very heavily for that error.'

Error. The poison had been in the water jug. I knew that. The door had been locked. The key had been on the other side of the door, out in the hall. I knew that, too. So Rivers had decided to draw the blinds over the situation. There was no murder attempt, and if not, there was nothing to tell the police. No need for cover stories, nothing. Why should a man want to conceal the fact that somebody had tried to kill him? And I knew the answer to that one, too. Because he was convinced it was Olivia. Somehow she'd got into the house, and fixed that jug. He still wanted to track her down his own way. I took a deep breath.

'You can't get away with this,' I told him evenly. 'That was no mistake. Somebody got that poison into you, and we both know it.'

'Mr Preston, whatever you may think, whatever theory you may have formed, I assure you that is precisely what happened. And Dr Hoskins will confirm that the medical evidence supports the fact that I swallowed the liquid by accident.

Isn't that right, Frank?'

But Hoskins wasn't paying attention. He was staring blankly at the floor, swallowing a lot, clenching his fists.

'Frank.'

Rivers's voice was sharp and commanding. The silent man looked across at him emptily.

'Oh sure,' he muttered. 'I agree, Barney. Absolutely.'

It was long odds he hadn't heard a word Rivers said. But it was clear that anything that had been said was O.K. with the distinguished doctor. Now Rivers banged on the desk.

'For God's sake, man. Pull yourself together. You're going to have to answer a lot of questions in a little while. What kind of an impression do you think you're going to make? Snap out of it.'

'He needs a drink, Mr Rivers.'

It was the first time Sam had spoken. Rivers swung his gaze around, to focus irritably on him.

'A drink? That is how he got into this state. He needs coffee, food. Not more of that muck.'

Thompson didn't want to fight. He looked at me.

'Sam is right,' I agreed. 'You're right too, Mr Rivers, but your remedy is long term. Weeks, months, maybe. You don't even have hours to play with. Short term, Sam is right. The man needs a good stiff drink. Let me show you.'

I went to where he kept his booze, poured out a half-tumbler of neat scotch, took it across to the trembling man. Not trusting it to his shaking hands, I held the glass to his lips. He sucked at it greedily, taking it down in great gulps. There were over four fingers in the glass. It was gone in less than ten seconds. Hoskins shook his head, shuddering violently. Strange sighing noises came from him, as he buried his face in his hands. After a few more seconds, he threw back his head, running fingers through his hair.

'Sorry Barney, I didn't quite catch that.'

The voice was normal, controlled. There was colour back on his cheeks. Rivers looked at me in astonishment. I shrugged. The man at the desk said: 'This accident here last night, Mr Preston thinks it might not have been an accident.'

'Not an accident?' echoed Hoskins. 'Nonsense. I've warned you a dozen times about keeping that stuff around where somebody might drink it by accident. But you wouldn't be told, not you. So, of course, the minute Preston described the situation on the telephone, I assumed at once it had finally happened. You're a lucky man, Barney. Don't deserve it. You ought to vote Mr Preston a little token of thanks, here. Something not too showy. Like the United Nations building, for example.'

He chuckled at his little joke. The bluff, hearty medical man. Laughing his genial way through the world of lesser mortals. I could have throttled him.

'And that's the way it'll be told,' I said flatly.

'Told? No need for anyone to be told anything at all, Mr Preston.' Rivers eyed me with a cold smile. 'A little household accident. I'm sure our policemen have quite enough to do without having to take notes every time someone cuts himself in the bathroom.'

'Oh absolutely,' boomed Hoskins. 'Busy guys, the police. Lot of respect for the police. No point in wasting their time.'

I knew I was licked. If that was the line they'd decided to adopt, there was no future in it for me to try contradicting them. And, like it or not, Rivers was my client.

'Then that's it. You ought to be more careful, Mr Rivers.'

The eyes that stared into mine held quiet triumph.

'You may rely on it. And now, I'm going to ask you and your associate to leave the house for a few hours. Dr Hoskins will be with me here, and the police will be coming out to see him. There will be quite enough of us present to cope with any situation which may arise. It would be an unnecessary complication for you gentlemen to be on the premises. Policemen are notoriously inquisitive, and they will be bound to wonder why you're here. This fire business is most annoying, and of course the doctor will be required to make a statement. But I can think of no valid reason why we involve the police in our little domestic affair here.'

What was it Lynda Lee said? Cold and remote. Or something of the kind. He was all that. Knowing I was going to be left holding the wrong end of an argument, I still came back at him.

'Mr Rivers. The sanatorium burned down last night. The same night Miss Hart promised you a fire. And it was her own prison, sorry hospital, that burned. The place where she'd been stuck these past years, the place she can have no reason to love. You're not seriously going to pretend she didn't do it.'

He was not pleased.

'I am not going to pretend anything. But neither am I going to jump to conclusions. What do I know of fires and their causes? This is work for professionals. Fire investigators, police officers. I'm sure they'll bring their best efforts to bear.'

'You could help them,' I insisted. 'You could say there's an escaped madwoman out there who's already threatened fire. You don't seriously imagine it wasn't her that did that, do you?'

It was Hoskins who replied.

'There is no question of that. And I resent your description of her as a madwoman. You seem to have an impression of some wild-eyed, imprecating harridan. Some medieval witch-type, with an insane preoccupation with arson. Olivia is not like that at all. She is a most intelligent, charming person. Most of the time. A person with a great regard for other people. It's true that she has a disturbed personality, which is why she is my patient. But the very thought of causing hurt and suffering to others, and I am referring to the other patients, not to mention the staff, this would be a totally repugnant concept to her. Even in her wildest moment. Wholly unacceptable. Whatever caused this disaster, it was not any act of hers. Out of the question.'

The conviction in his voice was not prompted by alcohol. Nor was it a matter of supporting his boss. I was hearing the balanced verdict of a man qualified to know. The words were still sinking in when Rivers came back into the attack, to press home the advantage.

'The position is no different from what it was when you and I first talked. A personal matter between Miss Hart and myself. It is my house which is threatened, and as a result possibly even the people in it. This other matter is unfortunate, but there is no connection. No more than a train smash or any other disaster. This one simply happens to be a little nearer home. Yesterday, I made it clear that the police were not to be involved. Nothing has changed.'

I knew I was going to have to take it. For now. And I could talk myself into accepting it. Whatever Olivia Hart may or may not have done at the sanatorium, it would only have been because of the connection with Rivers. She wasn't going to put the torch to the whole city. The next stop would be this house. If I told the law what I suspected they would probably stake out the place, and grab her. It would suit them fine, and I would be Joe Goodguy. But I wasn't hired for that. I was hired to do what Rivers wanted, and if I didn't, I didn't eat. I could stop the woman just as well as the lawmen, and at the same time, do what I was being paid to do.

Rivers watched me struggle with myself. I said: 'O.K. we'd better leave. I'll phone in a few hours to check if it's all right to come back out here.'

He smiled that thin smile of his.

'That would be most satisfactory.'

I motioned to Thompson, and we went outside, Larry following.

'Get our stuff in the car will you Sam. I just want a word with Larry.'

He shambled away. The boy walked beside me, waiting.

'Looks like we made a mistake last night,' I opened.

He shook his fair head in puzzlement.

'Guess so,' he agreed. 'I was kind of upset at the time. Maybe I jumped to the wrong conclusion.'

'Do you believe that?'

'I don't know,' he confessed. 'But hell, the old man ought to know what happened. He was the one who nearly died, after all. And there's something else, too.'

I stared at him hard.

'Something else?'

'Sure, obviously. Who'd want to do it? I mean, this place may not be Monkton Central, but it's not exactly deserted, either. Strangers can't just walk in and out without somebody seeing. And that would leave the people who aren't strangers, right? The people already here.'

I didn't altogether agree that it wouldn't be possible to get in and out without being seen. Difficult maybe, but not impossible. But I didn't want to argue.

'O.K. let's talk about those people. There's your sister and you.'

'Not guilty,' he grinned.

'The servants?'

'Old Pedro and Anna?' He chuckled. 'Just a couple of sweet old characters. I mean, you're really wasting your time there.'

That left only one possibility.

'Miss Nolan, then?'

'Aw come on, that'd be kind of stupid, wouldn't it?'

'How, stupid?'

'Why, if Kate's going to knock off the old man, surely she'll have sense enough to wait until she inherits the money?'

'The money,' I repeated, not understanding.

He stopped walking, and looked into my face.

'You don't know what I'm talking about, do you?'

'Maybe you'd better tell me,' I suggested.

'About Kate and the old man. They're getting married in two months from now.'

Well, well. In this world, a man learns all the time.

'No, I didn't know that,' I admitted.

'That explains it. So you can see, this is no time of year for our Kate to be bumping off the groom.'

'I guess not.'

There was something in the way he referred to 'our Kate' that prompted another question.

'How do you and Lynda Lee feel about it?'

'We're used to the idea now. I guess we were kind of resentful at first. Thought he was being disloyal to Judith. But, when I sat and thought about it, I could see his point of view. I mean, we may think he's a hundred years old, but he isn't really. He's forty-six. Probably has another thirty years to live, maybe more. That's a helluva long time to expect a man to sit around the house being loyal.'

A piece of perception that I wouldn't have expected from someone his age. His stock went up several points.

'You were fond of Judith, I gather.'

'Ah.' He sighed, and started walking again. 'She was the most. Don't mind telling you, Mr Preston, I was in love with that lady myself. Kid stuff. I was only eighteen, but I would have done anything for her.'

'Eighteen?' I queried. I was trying to adjust my time scale.

'When I first met her, I mean. I was twenty when — when it happened. I went sort of crazy for a while. Still, it's all a long time ago. In the past. Now, we're going to get Kate. And don't get me wrong. Kate is very much O.K. She's just not Judith.'

Outside the house, Sam Thompson waved.

'We'd better move out,' I said. 'I'll be back in a few hours. See you then.'

'Maybe. I'll probably go out some time today.'

'Well, see you sometime.'

The morning sun was strengthening up as I drove back into the city.

13

I went back to the Parkside to get freshened up. Frank, the dayman, looked me over as I went past.

'Good morning, Mr Preston.'

There was too much emphasis on that 'good', and something behind his broad grin I didn't care for. When I got into the apartment and inspected myself in the mirror, I could see his point. I looked like a sailor after a twenty-four hours stopover.

Thirty minutes later there was a definite improvement. Not as much as I would have liked, but I wouldn't be attracting any more grins.

Picking up the phone, I dialled a number and listened to some brr-brr before a voice said 'Monkton City Globe. Good morning.'

'Society Editor. Miss Blair.'

More noises, then a cool voice.

'Miss Blair, Who is this, please?'

I was glad I was clean and tidy. Which is a little ridiculous when you consider it was only a phone call.

'Mark Preston,' I told her, 'Good morning, Mike.'

The trouble with telephones is, you can't see facial reactions. Voices reaction was impersonal this time.

'Oh, hello. I hope you put the files back in order.'

'Neat and tidy,' I assured her. 'Thought I might return a favour. Was that on the level last night? When you said you were a big fan of the crime-columns?'

'Certainly.' Her tone said she was curious. 'Why?'

'There's a wedding coming up. Bernard L. Rivers, the husband of the woman who died in the accident. He's getting married again. A Miss Kathryn Nolan, his secretary. Did you know about it?'

'No. It's an item worth having. Thank you Mark. But I don't quite see the connection.'

'You would take it as normal, I imagine, to interview the bride? Talk

214

about clothes, honeymoon plans, stuff like that?'

'Yes. And — ?'

'Do it now. This minute. Get out to Rivers' house. Take a photographer. Quite by accident, you're going to stumble into an entirely different story. Front page, and exclusive. Especially exclusive. But it has to be right now.'

'You wouldn't lead a girl astray?' she demurred.

'At every available opportunity,' I assured her. 'But not over this, Mike. The paper will probably make you a V.I.P. Only you have to get on it pronto. And one other thing.'

'I'm listening.'

'Forget I told you. You're there on a fashion story. Just sheer coincidence you happened to be around. You don't even know me. Is it a deal?'

There was a rich velvet chuckle.

'Not quite. If this turns out the way it's beginning to sound, I shall be in your debt. I'm a girl who pays her debts. Ciao.'

'Good luck.'

She didn't leave me time to ask for

more detail on the debt situation. I could make of it what I liked. And I liked what I was making of it.

I took a ride over to the office. Florence Digby may have been surprised to see me, but she gave no sign.

'There is mail on your desk, Mr Preston. Nothing that can't wait.'

'Thank you. Any calls?'

She produced her pad, and began to report. The usual stuff had been filtering through while I was away. Florence was an expert with the filter business, and there was nothing for me to do.

'And one other. Mr Joshua Holland asked if you would call him when convenient.'

The way she spoke his name indicated that Mr Holland was very much O.K. with Miss Digby. Far more the type of person the office should be dealing with than most of the usual social categories she encountered. Miss Digby tries to bring a little dignity into the place, and although crime is my business, she much prefers it to be committed at a certain level. If she had her way, the body would always be found in the library.

'We'll get to him in a few minutes. Newspapers around?'

'Very much so.' She gave me a frosty appraisal. 'I imagine you will be aware already that Dr Hoskins' private clinic burned down last night?'

'Heard it on the radio,' I confirmed.

'Very strange it should have happened within hours of our enquiries on the doctor,' she insisted.

'Strange indeed,' I agreed. 'But don't look at me. I don't know any more about it than you do.'

I went through to my own office and closed the door. She'd told me it was O.K. to ignore the mail, and I never need any encouragement to do that. The papers were another matter. I settled down to them, searching for any scrap of information about the Hoskins fire. There wasn't much hard fact. A lot of good imaginative reporting, built around a hard core of information which told me little I didn't already know. I made a note of the names of the staff who'd been on duty at the time, which was two in the morning.

The blaze had originated in the administration building, which was separate from the residential and medical quarters. The man who died had not been identified, but was almost certainly some unfortunate derelict who sneaked into the place for a night's shelter. I toyed with the idea that Hoskins had put a match to the place himself. The business was running down, like the doctor himself. It would be a great temptation to pick up the insurance and have done with it. It was true he hadn't impressed me as being the arson type, but that was not very professional thinking. What did I mean by an arson type? It made about as much sense as a murder type. Anybody with strength enough to pull a trigger is a murder type. Anybody who can strike a match can commit arson. Little kids do it every day.

My eyes began to stray to the racing section, and I knew I'd finished reading the papers. Regretfully, I pushed them to one side, and put a call through to Holland.

'Josh? Preston,' I announced. 'What gives?'

'Ah yes,' he recalled. 'I had an odd telephone conversation about you. Hope I've done the right thing.'

Very helpful.

'I'll have to hear it before I'd know,' I prompted.

'Of course. Well now, you were interested in obtaining a copy of a Westley portrait. I'm told there is one.'

I became very wide awake.

'That's great news. Can you get it for me?'

His voice became guarded.

'Let me tell you what happened. You remember meeting a little guy called Phil?'

Guy. So it had been male.

'I wasn't sure whether it was male or female,' I confessed.

'That's the one. A terrible busybody, as you may have gathered. Not above listening to other peoples conversations.'

Who is?

'And — '

'He listened to you asking Nigel Bravington about the Judith Rivers portrait. Nigel denied any copy. But Phil says there is one. He's seen it. Went up to Nigel's little place upstairs one time. The door had been left open, which is not usual. He saw Nigel sitting there, just staring at this picture of a woman. From his description, it has to be the one. Either that, or you're on the track of a missing Westley. In which case, you have a guaranteed place in the future history of art.'

'A missing Westley?' I repeated. 'Is it possible?'

He laughed shortly.

'It's always possible. But the rumours don't usually begin to circulate until a painter's been dead fifty years. Personally, I doubt it very much. We're not talking about some romantic figure who died in an attic over in Europe three hundred years ago. This was Westley, late twentieth century man, fully documented. The guy would have trouble buying a new brush that wasn't known about, leave alone painting secret portraits. No, for my money it's a copy. Thought you should know.'

'You're right, and thanks.'

'Had to promise the little man twenty dollars.'

'You got it. Anything else I should know?'

We talked for another few minutes and I put down the phone. A copy of the Rivers portrait. I had to see it, touch it. And, unless someone was going to prevent it, I was determined to have it for myself. So Bravington had been holding out on me. It was no surprise. People do it all the time. But I was puzzled as to why. All he needed to say was that he had a copy, and it was not for sale. That would have stopped me cold. This way, he made everything complicated.

I told Florence I'd be out at Rivers Bend in a few hours time, and left the office. At the Tattered Canvas, the assorted bird-life had assembled for the midday twitter. The little man Phil was not on view. He was probably out spending the twenty, my twenty, before these other characters found out he had it.

Nigel was leaning on the counter, speaking in a low voice to a tubby man with a pigtail. Beside him was a tall glass, with an inch of liquid in the bottom, and most of a fruit crop filling the rest. Maybe that's what people mean when they talk about taking lunch out of a glass.

If he was pleased to see me, he concealed it well.

'Hello.' The voice was dull, uninterested.

'Hi,' I returned. 'Could you spare a minute?'

'It's a busy time,' he objected.

I nodded.

'So I see. I'll be sure not to keep you from your lovely friends too long.'

He shrugged with mild annoyance.

'Keep an eye on things, Adrian dear. Make sure they can pay before they have any drinkies. And especially that bunch in the corner. I mean, they are too devastatingly broke. Very boring.'

Adrian dear nodded, and his pigtail almost landed in a glass of some green fluid. Nigel came around the counter.

'Well?'

'Upstairs would be best.'

He clucked with annoyance and led the

way. And yet in spite of his obvious irritation, there seemed to be some other thing on his mind. Was I inventing it, or was there just a small slump to the shoulders?

Upstairs, he motioned me into the room where we'd sat the day before, and closed the door. The man was clearly under some kind of strain, and it showed on his face. Last time I'd thought he was about twenty five years old, but now it was clear I'd been wrong. He was closer to thirty.

Douglas Westley's portrait took in the way we stood looking at each other. It was unnerving to realise he wouldn't give a damn if we started to cut one another into fragments.

'You said this would be brief. I'm holding you to it,' snapped Nigel.

I jerked a thumb at the picture.

'Should have asked you before. Is that a self-portrait, or did you do it?'

The question was unexpected, but not unwelcome. He even contrived a half-grin.

'A very flattering question. Matter of

fact, I did it myself. I'm really rather proud of it. Even a few experts have thought Douglas could have been the painter.'

'Mind if I take a closer look?'

Without waiting for an answer I went over and peered into the canvas. But it was the edging I was studying. I lifted the picture off the wall and turned round.

'Hey, wait a — '

'Daylight,' I explained. 'Like to get a different slant on the face.'

I rested the picture flat on a table, where the sun streamed through, lighting it up. Bravington clearly thought I was crazy. I hoped he was wrong. Taking a deep breath, I slid fingers under the framed edging and exerted pressure. The frame began to separate.

'Stop that.'

He rushed over, putting a hand on my arm.

'What are you doing, for God's sake? You'll tear the picture. Are you mad?'

I took my hands away, and stood clear.

'That was worrying me,' I admitted. 'Not knowing just how it's fixed, I could have torn that canvas. Wouldn't want to do that.'

'Well then?'

'But it does lift away, Nigel. You know how to do it properly. Maybe you'd better do it yourself. Or shall I carry on?'

I crossed my fingers that Josh Holland's information was the real stuff.

About to protest, he saw there was no room for argument on my face. Reluctantly he placed slim fingers at the sides of the picture, running them expertly up and down, pressing. The small split I'd started became a gap. He took one last look at me.

'It has to come off.'

I was feeling excitement now. Douglas Westley's face came away in his hands, complete in its own half inch thick frame. Beneath it was another picture. A picture of a woman, with the sun bouncing off radiant golden hair.

14

I stared at Judith's face again, mesmer-
ised the way I'd been the last time, when
she looked down at me from her little
fortress out at Rivers Bend. Then I
realised I'd been mistaken that last time.
At this new angle, her expression seemed
somehow different. More knowing. She
wasn't the way I'd remembered. I wished
the picture was high up on a wall, so that
what seemed like a new expression would
soften again with the movement of the
room shadows.

'So you know.'

Nigel was still holding the other
canvas. For a few seconds, I'd almost
forgotten he was there. His face was a
strange mixture of defiance, resignation,
despair, and who could tell what. It
seemed to me he was making a lot of
fuss out of being trapped in one fairly
small lie. After all, if he didn't want to
tell me he had a copy of Judith's portrait,

there was no law to say he had to.

I ignored him, getting back to my inspection of her face, and regretting again that I was seeing it from this new angle.

'How did you find out?'

His voice was tense, and it was obvious he was working himself up. I put it down to artistic temperament, whatever that is.

'Does it matter?' I countered.

Temperament or no, he was very careful in the way he set down the Westley picture in a safe position. Then he dropped down into a chair, ashen-faced.

'Matter?' he echoed. 'No, I don't suppose it does. Not really. In a way, I guess it's some kind of relief that it's all over.'

If he wanted to tell me a story about the copy, I was more than willing to hear it. I'd listen to anybody who wanted to talk about Judith Harvey Rivers. So I sat down across from him, and stuck an Old Favourite in my mouth.

'You want to tell me about it? From your viewpoint?'

He shrugged helplessly.

'Does my view matter?'

'Well, for God's sake, you'd better have one.'

I was getting annoyed with all this pussy-footing around over a simple matter.

'Yes, yes you're right. I'd better have one. If I leave it to the fertile brain of that cold-hearted bastard, I'll find myself in death row in no time flat.'

A gleaming coal from the cigarette dropped onto the back of my wrist, but I didn't dare to flinch. Cold-hearted bastard? Death row? My mind scurried around, looking for impersonal words.

'Now you're thinking more clearly,' I said, with great care. 'You must have your own version.'

Not bad, I decided. When you don't know what the conversation is about, the best contribution is complete silence. Next best are words that don't disturb the flow. He looked at me oddly.

'You're a strange character. Shouldn't you be waving a gun around, and screaming for policemen?'

'Probably,' I conceded. 'But I find it

makes people all excited. It upsets them. Personally, I go for the quiet chat approach. It's more soothing all around.'

I was warming to my part. Now, he chuckled. True, it was a strained, desperate kind of sound, but an undeniable chuckle.

'I told you before, you remind me a little of Douglas. If he was sitting there, he'd be saying 'Why don't we all have a nice cup of coffee, and talk it through'.'

I inclined my head.

'Why don't we take his advice? Without the coffee.'

The idea of Nigel loose in that kitchen, where the big forty-five lived, held no appeal. He waved his arms about.

'Where do I start?'

I pointed to where Judith rested on the table.

'That's what caused all the bother. Let's start with that.'

'I still don't understand how you found out about that. I swore to him I'd destroyed it.'

'It doesn't matter how I found out,' I

reminded him. 'All that matters is, I know.'

'Very well. Let's start with the portrait. Tell me honestly, and I know you're not a connoisseur, but could you have brought yourself to burn such a picture? I mean, even leaving to one side the fact that it's a genuine Westley? No, I can see by your face, you couldn't.'

If that's what he could see on my face, let him think it. What he really saw was some change of expression at the words he used. Genuine Westley? Genuine? And I knew it was true, even as he spoke. That shift of expression about the mouth. Was it mockery? Looseness? I didn't know. But now I knew it wasn't the new position, not the angle I was looking at the picture. It wasn't the changed shadow. Or the sunlight. It was a different picture entirely. A picture with a flaw. A genuine Westley.

'To use your own words, I'm no connoisseur. So I'll go for the version up at the house.'

He nodded.

'It's a good piece of work. I'm not

going to be bashful about it. I'm a professional, after all. And the star pupil. It's to be expected I would produce a good job. But that's all it is. A job. A pretty picture, done to order, to please the guy who pays the tab. Years ago, the artist had to make the picture flatter the king, or the nobleman, or whoever. If he loused it up, he might find himself on the rack. We don't seem to have moved along very far, do we?'

The part of the king will be played by Bernard L. Rivers, I mused.

'You were going to give me your side of the story,' I reminded.

'Yes.' He ran his fingers through the thick fair hair, and there was pleading on his face. 'It was an accident, you know. I could never have killed him, whatever I threatened.'

My expression was non-commital.

'Go on.'

'I went to the studio in a hell of a state. I was going to have it out with him about the woman. About her.' His head jerked towards Judith's picture. 'With the others, he could always laugh me out of it. I was

231

the only one who really mattered to him, you know. It had always been that way. When he'd been with one of his — his creatures he would come and tell me all about it. I'd be jealous of course, but we'd wind up laughing, because really they didn't matter. We were what mattered, Douglas and me. What we had was special, something that couldn't be touched by those simpering cows. I would forgive him, and he'd cook for us, and we'd make up.'

Although I felt a certain revulsion, it was tinged somehow with a kind of pity for the tormented man opposite.

'But he couldn't laugh off this one?' I queried.

'No. With her, it seemed somehow different. She was beginning to get to him. One can always tell, you know. Little things can tell a whole lot, when you're really tuned in to somebody. And if I'm to be honest with you, I could almost understand why. She wasn't like the others. Not looking for some cheap adventure with the famous artist. I was certain she really was in love with him.

And it was starting to have an effect. He stopped being so open with me. There'd be a small lie sometime, and I would find out. I kept telling myself there was nothing to worry about. He would come around, things would be back to normal. But I didn't really believe it. That night I had a lot to drink. I'm not much of a drinker, it always makes me miserable. But I had one too many, and worked myself up into a rage. I decided to go and have it out with him. There was a row.'

He stopped talking for a moment, remembering. Not daring to interrupt, I stared across at the portrait of Westley. He stared back, through me, past me. Unmoved.

Bravington shook himself, as if to shake his mind free.

'A terrible row. I was pleading one moment, threatening the next. Douglas made no attempt to conciliate me. None. He just laughed. Really laughed at me. At first, that is. Then he got angry, as well. We were like two cats in an alley. Spitting, snarling, walking round each other. He had this gun, had it for years. He pulled it

233

out of a drawer and said he'd kill himself, if I didn't stop. It was just like him. Always pulling some dramatic stunt. First of all, he said he'd shoot himself in the — well, down where the trouble was. Then he changed his mind. He'd blow out his brains. Actually put the gun to his head. He was only enjoying himself really. But I wasn't. I was shouting, screaming at him to go ahead. I wanted him to. But he changed his mind again. After all, he said, his heart was broken already. A little bullet wouldn't make much difference. So — so, he put the gun to his heart. I jumped at him.'

He stopped talking, and looked over at me, with misery big on his face.

'You jumped at him,' I prodded.

'M'm, yes.' He got quickly to his feet, and paced around. 'I promised you the truth. But the fact is, from here on I don't really know what the truth is. Why did I go towards him? Was it to take the gun away? Or was it to make him do it? Make him kill himself? I've relived it a thousand times, a million times. And still I don't know. I grabbed his hand, and the gun went off. Just once. He looked at me, and his face was very strange. He tried to say something, but he couldn't. He just fell down. Dead.'

I kept very quiet. Bravington couldn't take that.

'Well?'

The story of the way Westley died had given me too much to think about. In my mind, there had been wonderings. Suspicions about little things I'd seen or heard. Even some kind of half-formed theory had begun to shape itself, an explanation for all the odd events that seemed to follow the death of Douglas Westley. This new information, about the stupid and needless way the man had died, had wiped the slate. I would have to start over.

'Aren't you going to say anything?'

The man looking at me was on the verge of becoming hysterical.

'I was thinking about what you just told me,' I said slowly. 'Mulling it over. And I was waiting to hear the rest.'

'What difference does it make, the rest of it?' His voice was broken. 'Douglas was dead. Nothing could matter after that.'

'Wrong,' I contradicted. 'It all has to come out now. No more hiding away. Let's say I believe you. Never mind anybody else's version.'

A fair point to start from. There was no need to complicate this by telling him I hadn't heard any other version. The look on his face was strange.

'Believe me?' he echoed. 'Even if you did, what difference would that make? You're working for him. He pays you. You'll do what he says, the way everybody does.'

At least I could react to that, with some feeling.

'Sure, he pays me. And up to a point, I will always go along with the man who meets the tab. But I'm not going to be paid to railroad somebody into the death house. If that's where you belong, the law will put you there. If you think I'm going to suppress information which might keep you out, you have me wrong.'

He'd been grinding the heels of his hands together. Now he stopped, searching my face with his eyes.

'You mean it?'

'Certainly I mean it,' I snapped. 'But I can't act without knowing what I'm doing. As of now, I am withholding information about a possible homicide. No matter how long ago it happened, I suddenly find myself an accessory after the fact. Technically. So you'd better tell me the rest, and fast. Let's say I'm prepared to believe you about what happened. When a man dies that way, people do one of several things. They kill themselves, they scream for the law, they run away. What did you do?'

'I went out to kill her. To kill Judith.'

Naturally. In his mind, Westley's death would have been her fault.

'Go on.'

'Out to the house. I was completely out of control. How I ever drove the car there without hitting anything is a mystery to me.'

'And you took the gun?' I shot in.

'Gun? No. Didn't give it a thought. I didn't want any gun, or a knife or anything else that would come between us. It had to be personal. Me and her. I was going to strangle her, kick her to death, tear pieces off her body with my hands.'

There was a strange light in his eyes as he relived the feeling.

'You went to the house.'

'Drove like a mad thing all the way. At first, I thought the house was empty. I ran into every room, screaming her name. Then I found him, Rivers. He was alone there, in that study of his. As I threw open the door, he simply sat there, looking at me.'

'Did you attack him?'

'No. No, quite the reverse. The study was my last chance of finding Judith. I knew she was nowhere else around. When I saw her husband, all the energy seemed to drain out of me. Attack him? How could I? As things stood, I felt nothing but pity for the poor guy. We were in the same fix, after all, even though he didn't know it. She'd betrayed the pair of us. No, I didn't attack him. I sat down in a chair, and cried.'

In my mind's eye I could see the picture. Rivers at his desk, looking up from his work at the sudden intrusion. The wild-eyed man rushing in, collapsing in front of him. The unhurried reaction.

'How did he react?' I asked.

'Oh, he was very good with me. Very kind. He calmed me down, gave me a glass of water, talked to me like a dutch uncle. Oh yes, he was very good to me, or so I thought. I told him everything, you know.'

'Did he mention the police?'

'Yes. Very clever about that. He said the police would have to be involved, but that I was in no shape to talk to them at that moment in time. He believed it was an accident, but the way I was behaving I would talk myself straight into a death sentence. What I needed was a couple of hours rest. Get myself into a more reasonable frame of mind. Time enough then to talk to the police. At that moment, he could have done anything he liked with me. I was so grateful, you've no idea. Grateful.'

He repeated the word, and the bitterness in his tone was like a sting.

'So you followed his advice.'

'It made sense. Even in my worked-up state, I could tell that. He gave me a sedative, and put me in a bedroom to lie down for a while. I was asleep about three hours. For him, it must have been a very busy time.'

I smoked steadily, saying nothing. My mind was a turmoil of activity. Facts had to be reassessed, categorised anew. Sequences which had seemed at least half-acceptable now had to be broken up and reassembled. Even as I tried to do it, I knew it was largely a waste of time. Bravington hadn't finished his story yet. When I'd heard it all, that would be the time for the big reappraisal. Now was the time for smoking, and keeping an uninvolved expression.

'A lot can be done in three hours,' I said pointlessly.

He nodded gravely, as though I'd made an important contribution.

'Particularly if you have a fast brain, a heart like ice, and zillions in the bank. Rivers had it all cut and dried. I stood no chance against him. I'd like you to believe that. And, as you will realise, with the urgency gone out of me, I was all set to look at things differently.'

I realised better than he knew. The pattern was classic, and always will be. In the heat of the moment, people will do things, say things. Take out the heat, let in some daylight, and you have a whole new ballgame. Especially when the question of self-preservation is involved.

'What did Rivers have to say?'

'He had it all worked out. He'd been to the studio, to check what I'd said. There was nothing to indicate that Douglas hadn't taken his own life. Why not leave it alone? Here was I, at the beginning of a great career, an important career. What would it serve the world if I ruined all that? I had suffered enough. At first, I wanted to argue, we must have talked for an hour, just on that one point. But I learned something. When a man is arguing to his own disadvantage, arguing in favour of ruining his own life, he doesn't argue hard enough, Mark. Basically, he's ready to be persuaded.'

'Right,' I agreed. 'They call it survival.'

The painter wagged his head sadly.

241

'Once I'd agreed on that, the rest followed. Rivers pointed out that Westley had ruined his life as well. After a decent interval, he would divorce Judith. We were in the same boat, he and I. Would you believe, I actually felt sorry for the guy? When he wanted something in return, I was only too willing to listen.'

I pointed to the lady with the golden hair.

'He wanted you to do an imitation portrait. Without the famous Westley flaw.'

'Yes. Douglas had only finished the picture a few days earlier. Rivers was furious. Said it made Judith look brazen, somehow. He certainly would not accept it. And of course Douglas being Douglas, was adamant that it must stand as it was.'

'And now,' I was thinking aloud, 'there was this changed position. Westley was gone, but the star pupil was still alive. Alive, and in Rivers' debt.'

'I didn't want to do it,' he assured me. 'I'm a creative artist, an original, not a hack. But I agreed. And there was one other thing. He wanted to safeguard my legal position. It might be necessary one day for me to defend myself over Douglas' death. He'd brought a doctor to the house. He would examine me, and make a record of my emotional condition. This doctor, who was his friend Hoskins of course, had no idea of the circumstances, and there would be no mention of why he was giving me this physical. Rivers stressed that very hard, said if the doctor was aware of the facts, he could be accused later of conspiracy. I could understand that, and we didn't exchange more than a dozen words.'

'And after that, you went down to Baja California,' I finished.

He looked astonished.

'How did you know that?'

'You told me. Yesterday,' I reminded. 'Something about the sunset down there.'

'So I did,' he remembered. 'Well, that was it. When I came back, Judith Rivers was dead. The papers all said it was an accident. Rivers saw me when I got home. He said he realised that I would know at once there hadn't been an accident. Judith had killed herself quite deliberately, because of what she thought was Douglas' suicide. But he begged me to keep out of it. Let it be an accident. If it came out that she'd killed herself, there'd be questions as to the reason. They were both gone now. They'd caused enough unhappiness, without adding to it. It all sounded like good, sane reasoning. I agreed, as he'd known I would. It was all over. I got on with my own life.'

But I wasn't satisfied yet.

'I can understand what you've said so far. It all makes sense, except that you keep on referring to Rivers as if he were an enemy. I think if I'd been in his spot, and had his kind of money, I could well have done what he did. Certainly he didn't harm you. Why are you so against him?'

'Oh, I wasn't. Not for a long time. Not until that business with young Patti Dean.'

Patti Dean? Click.

'The girl in the paternity case against Rivers' son. A year ago?'

'That's the one. That child was

railroaded. I'm by way of being a hero with the art-course youngsters. I know a lot of what goes on. In her case there were bribes, false evidence, a whole lot of money spread around. It being his son, I took a special interest. I realised what he was doing. There was nothing I could do about it. But I could think. Now that I could watch him operate on someone else, and from a distance, I could take another look at what he'd done in the past. I knew then that Judith hadn't taken her own life. She was murdered. I went to him, and he laughed in my face. No more of the kindly uncle. I could think what the hell I liked. Nobody was going to listen to me, not against him. He went over Douglas' death again. Pointed out that I'd concealed evidence from the law, as a minimum charge. And what would the police make of it, when they learned I'd gone straight to a doctor, to have it recorded that I was not emotionally responsible on that day? He'd tricked me into that, but I could never prove it. I was helpless all around, just a man with a lot of words.'

He was right about that.

'And so there was nothing you could do?'

'Nothing,' he agreed. 'Nothing then, nothing since. Just live with it all, and try to carry on. Until yesterday, that is. When you showed up here. It brought everything back, with a rush. I was very frightened. I was certain it was him again, up to something. Plotting. Then, when the Hoskins place burned down last night, I was more positive than ever. I don't pretend to understand his motives, what makes it necessary to raise all this again after years have gone by. But it's Rivers. I know it is, and I'm afraid.'

In his position I could understand that.

'You haven't told me about Olivia Jayne Hart.'

His face was startled.

'Who?'

And the combination of his expression and his tone explained why.

'Forget it. What's your relationship with Lynda Lee?'

'I don't have one,' he replied. 'She's just one of the kids. What makes you ask?'

'You let her borrow your car last night,' I accused.

'Oh, that's where it went. Lots of people borrow my car, when they can't get home.'

'Do lots of them crash it up?' I persisted.

Now he was concerned.

'A crash? Is she all right?'

'She had a drunk's luck. But the car doesn't look too good.'

He shrugged.

'Rivers will pay. I shan't lose any sleep. This other girl you mentioned, this Olivia something, was she in the crash, too?'

'No. Forget her. The two don't connect. Listen carefully, because the police have already talked with Hoskins today. I don't think he'll have raked up the past at all. Rivers has too tight a rein on him. But it's all going to be very delicate the next few hours, even days. You and I had better understand each other.'

He leaned forward, listening.

15

Dr Franklyn Hoskins was listed at an address half a mile from his sanatorium. Far enough away that he couldn't hear the patients, close enough that he could reach the place in five minutes if he was needed. I drove past the house once, checking for police cars, but the only car on view was the three year old sedan he'd driven out to Rivers Bend.

I came back again, and drove in. He must have been watching for visitors, because the door opened before I could knock. The good doctor was very composed, so I imagined the liquor level was being maintained.

'You'd better let me come in, doctor,' I told him. 'A few things we have to get straight.'

He didn't argue, but walked back inside, leaving the door open. I followed him into a room furnished with the kind of spartan comfort of a man who lives by himself. There was a half-empty fifth of scotch standing on a table. No glass. I dropped into an adjacent chair.

'How'd it go with the police?' I opened.

'They were very courteous,' he replied. 'Very formal though. After all, the place is insured for six hundred thousand.'

'Wow. Does that money come to you?'

He looked at me narrowly.

'You have no right to ask me questions like that. As a matter of fact, no. There is a board of trustees. No one puts the cash in his pocket, if that's what you mean. It will have to be used to rebuild.'

'That must have been a good point with the law.'

'They certainly seemed to thaw out, once they heard it. But there is still this poor old devil who died.'

I nodded.

'Agreed. But if there's no question of profit, and therefore no arson, he just becomes another accidental death. I mean, it's tough and all that, but they can't expect you to guard against vagrants. Did they ask about anything else?'

'What else is there?' he queried, and his tone was guarded.

I shrugged off-handedly.

'Oh, could be any old thing. Judith for example. Weren't they curious about why old Barney murdered his wife?'

He looked at me very hard, for a long moment. Then he took a stiff pace towards the desk. I reached over quickly, and grabbed the bottle, shoving it down beside me in the chair.

'You don't want to drink that nasty old stuff when we're talking. In any case I wouldn't have expected a little chat about murder to upset you. Not with all your experience.'

He sat down, where he could see the bottle.

'I don't understand a word you're saying.'

'Oh yes, you do. It'll all come back. Concentrate. First of all, Nigel Bravington bumped off Westley. Judith and the great artist had been doing some haymaking, and Bravington didn't like it. You gave him a physical a few hours later, so you could testify he was of unsound mind. If it ever cropped up, that is. Then, to make everything tidy all round, good old Barney got rid of Judith. You must have thought that was highly suspicious, even if you couldn't prove anything. I'm surprised the police haven't talked to you about all these little details. Maybe it's because they don't know. Not yet. But they will, never fear. I'm going to tell them. Well, I won't keep you, doctor. You probably have a busy schedule, covering up murders and so forth.'

I made to get up.

'Wait.'

His tone was urgent. Imperative. It sounded odd, coming from a face which had begun to twitch. Trembling fingers pointed to the scotch.

'Could I just — ?'

'Not a chance. Mustn't be all sleepy when the boys from the homicide bureau drop in. Wouldn't be polite.'

He sat, hunched up, picking at his wrist with nervous fingers.

'You're meddling in things you don't understand.'

'I've done it before,' I assured him.

<hr />

251

'Yes, but you're quite wrong.'

He'd been about to say something else, but he changed his mind, and his lips set in a determined line.

'I often am,' I told him breezily. 'It doesn't bother me. And if I'm wrong, well, there's no harm in my telling the police.'

His movement was so fast, it almost worked. He flung himself headlong towards me, and actually got one hand around the bottle before I'd reacted enough to plant an open hand against his chest.

'No,' I said nastily. 'We'll just sit around here for an hour or two. All day, if we have to. Or maybe it would speed things up if I just poured this stuff out of the window.'

I stood, holding the bottle, and walked towards an open window.

'No, no.'

He sat on the floor, shaking his head, and sobbing. I felt sorry for him. But I felt sorrier for the dead.

'Better make up your mind, Hoskins. This way, you lose.'

'All right, all right.' His voice was full of anxious hope. 'Just give me a small one and — '

'Nothing,' I said brutally.

Even then, he fought against talking. He bit at his mouth, and a small trickle of blood ran down his chin.

'Listen,' he muttered. 'Barney Rivers is a very rich man. He's done nothing wrong, not really wrong. You've stumbled into things you don't understand. This nonsense about Bravington having killed Westley. It just is not true. I don't know where you got such an idea.'

'From him. From Bravington himself,' I replied. 'A man doesn't usually get confused about committing murder.'

The rolling eyes tried to gear themselves into focus.

'Bravington said that?'

He didn't believe a word of it.

'An hour ago. He told me all about it.'

Keeping my voice matter-of-fact, I went through the story, the way Nigel Bravington had told it to me. Hoskins sat quietly, but he couldn't control the twitching. Every now and then he would

253

shake his head, as if he was about to contradict me. Gradually, the impulse to interrupt faded away. The head-shaking continued, but now it was different. Now it was no longer the impatient need to correct errors in the story. It became the unwilling acceptance of what he was being told.

'Well, that's it doctor. Strictly speaking, none of it is any of my concern. The two principals have been dead so long, so many facts have disappeared or been altered, I doubt whether the police will even prosecute. But they have to be told. Can't have all these killers roaming the streets without the lawmen at least knowing who they are. It's kind of bad luck on Rivers, in a way. If he hadn't been so scared that somebody might set fire to that picture, he'd never have called me in. None of this need ever have come out. And, talking about fire, I'll have to tell the law about Olivia, too. Or are you going to tell me your place burned down by accident? She has to be found, and stopped. She already killed one man, whether she meant to or not.'

'No. No, you still don't understand. I'm only just beginning to understand it myself. But I still think he acted with only the best of motives. It was just that he was so convinced Judith had killed Westley. She had to be protected from that. She wasn't really responsible, not in the legal sense. He wanted me to help save her from some state institution. I could see nothing wrong with that.'

I sneered.

'Didn't it strike you as odd when he killed her? Or got somebody else to do it for him? I don't know the details, but he was responsible, I'll bet on that.'

'I think you'd better come with me.'

He rose unsteadily, and I did the same. Despite the shaking, there was a faint authority back in his voice. A sureness. We didn't say any more as he led me out. Across the hall, he opened a door into another room, where heavy curtains kept out the glare of the sun. In a tall, winged chair, a woman sat, hands folded. My eyes were still adjusting to the gloom.

'I've brought someone to see you.'

Hoskins' voice was low, kindly. 'Nothing to be afraid of.'

She looked round at me. In that light, she could have been anywhere between thirty and fifty years old.

'Mr Preston, here's someone you should meet. This is Judith Harvey Rivers.'

★　★　★

When I parked at the foot of those stone steps, I was harking back to my first visit to Rivers Bend. That time the view had been enhanced by one nymph perched on the stone balustrade. Otherwise everything was the same. Neat, orderly, musical accompaniment from the playing fountain. I still couldn't bring myself to check on those fish.

As I reached the open front door I heard the sound of another car turning into the driveway.

There was no need to look round. I knew who it would be.

The family members were all waiting in the study. Larry, leaning against the open window. Lynda Lee, sitting down and thumbing through an expensive magazine. Behind the desk, watching me come, sat Bernard L. Rivers.

'Ah, there you are.' The voice was controlled. Naturally. 'As you see, we're all here. Why the children should be involved, I can't see, but you wanted them to hear about it. Mr Preston has something very important to tell us.'

The young people looked over at me with interest. I draped myself in a chair, and looked at each in turn.

'That I do,' I confirmed. 'You probably know by now, your father has been afraid someone might set fire to this house. You can all relax. I've located that someone, and I'm satisfied there's nothing to fear.'

Rivers looked anything but happy. The others were full of interest.

'Well, go on man. There has to be more. How can you be so certain?'

This from Larry. I said gravely.

'The woman who was supposed to be the unseen enemy is tucked away in a graveyard. In New York. She's been dead four years. Her name was Olivia Jayne Hart.'

A bug droned in through the window. Rivers picked up a king-sized aerosol can and squirted at it. The very normality of the action struck a false note.

'Dead? Four years?' Larry looked and sounded bewildered. 'I don't get it.'

'Neither did I,' I assured him. 'It took a while. It all goes back to Judith. She fell in love with the man who painted her portrait, Douglas Westley. Westley killed himself — '

'That's a lie,' Rivers interrupted, but still in a calm voice. 'She killed him. Judith. I don't know what else you're going to say, but you'd better know that.'

'Judith murdered someone? I don't believe it,' exclaimed Lynda Lee.

I held up a hand.

'Wait a minute. Let me tell it. You're right, Lynda Lee. Judith didn't kill Westley, but your father wanted her out of the way. She had committed a crime much worse than murder, in his book. She fell in love with someone else, and that had to be punished.'

'Punished?' Larry interjected. 'Are you saying that Judith's death was no accident? That my father killed her?'

'Oh, no,' I denied. 'Not a bit of it. Murderers can get caught. She had to be punished, but not in any way that he might have to suffer for later. He put her away. He called in his old doctor buddy, Hoskins, and persuaded him that she'd killed Westley. Naturally, she was in a highly distressed state over the death, Hoskins was ready to believe what he was told. Your dear kind father was only acting in her best interests, after all. It was the choice between good care and treatment in a private sanatorium, and whatever kind of alternative she could expect in the state funny farm. You couldn't really blame the doctor for being fooled. He thought he was being a humanitarian.'

'But Judith — ' began Lynda Lee.

'In a moment,' I stopped her. 'Kate Nolan came along, and your father decided to get married again. He's a very marrying kind of man. But Hoskins knew that he already had one wife, very much alive — '

'Alive.' This was a chorus from both the Rivers offspring.

'Oh, yes. That made it all untidy. Your father decided to have a lunatic escape from custody, and try to burn down this house. I don't know what the final scene would have been, but I have a nasty feeling I was elected for the job of killing the intruder. Even if he had to do it himself, I would certainly be, at the very least, a first-class unbiased witness. A patient of Dr Hoskins, by name Olivia Jayne Hart, would be dead. All very unfortunate, but knowing the way he operates, I'm sure it would be explained to the satisfaction of the law people.'

Rivers' voice was flat and almost devoid of expression.

'I don't believe I've ever heard so much rubbish in such a short time. You forget you were here when Olivia telephoned.'

'No,' I contradicted. 'I was here when the phone rang, that's all. You're an electronic buff, you told me so yourself. It doesn't take any genius to make a phone bell ring.'

'And what about the poison in the

water jug?' he persisted. 'I know I tried to cover it up as a suicide attempt, but you knew I wasn't telling the truth.'

I nodded.

'Yes, that had me going, I admit. A double bluff, and I fell for it.'

'The door was locked from outside. You said so.'

'I was wrong. The key was outside, that much I knew. But I've looked at the door since. There's a gap at the bottom. It's wide enough to push a key through, and flick it a few feet away. Once you did that, all you needed to do was lie on the floor, with a mouthful of the stuff, and wait until you were quite certain we were coming in. Probably when I shot off the lock. You never were in any danger, but you had a well-authenticated murder attempt if you should need to use it. After you'd killed the woman people thought was Olivia.'

Larry's voice was strangely subdued.

'But the body, Judith's body?'

'Was identified by him. Check with the coastguard. Within a stretch of fifty miles either way, an average of three bodies a week, every week, gets washed ashore. A lot of them are young women, and a lot are Jane Does. It was only a matter of waiting for one that would pass as Judith. A few days in the water make identification very difficult.'

Rivers got to his feet. His attitude was not threatening, but I thought I ought to stand as well. Just in case.

'I imagine you got most of this fairy tale from that drunken fool Hoskins. Not much of a witness. And you forget something. Even if it were all true, I would have committed no crime. I think you'd better get out now. Needless to say, I shall not pay any bill you send me.'

You had to give it to the guy. No panic. No gun-waving. Just icy detachment.

'There's another bill coming your way,' I told him. 'From the people of the State of California. And I have to admit, it's real bad luck. You had to destroy all the evidence about Olivia Jayne Hart. Fingerprints, personal items. But you didn't want to hurt innocent people. You decided to have a fire, but to arrange it so there would be plenty of time for everyone to get free. You did a good job, too. It must have been an unpleasant surprise when you found out about the poor chump who died. A total stranger. All the evil things you've been responsible for, and the law can't prove a thing. Some old derelict gets wined up, and you take the fall. Ironic, wouldn't you say?'

'Flights of fancy. You'll really have to do something about that imagination.'

He walked past me to the door.

'And the picture, too,' I reminded. 'The fake Westley. You'll have a swell time explaining that.'

Rivers ignored me, and left the study. We all trooped along, into the hall. Hoskins, and a frightened middle-aged woman stood there.

Lynda Lee said incredulously,
'Judith?'

Then she ran over and took her in her arms. They were both weeping. Above their heads, the curtains swished back, then the shutters rolled.

I stood, trapped again by the magic of the portrait, as Judith Harvey Rivers gazed serenely down. I couldn't bring myself to look at the weeping figure a few feet away. That wasn't Judith. Not my Judith.

'A fake you say?'

Rivers stood beneath the picture, looking up. Suddenly the aerosol can was in his hand. My mind worked too slowly. A lighter snapped and a four foot flame leaped from the can. He played it directly onto her face. Horrible scorch marks appeared, then flame, burning, blackening that gorgeous hair, the eyes. I leaped at him, knocking the can away. It sputtered on the floor, but I hadn't been quick enough.

All that remained was blackened canvas.

From outside came the wail of a police siren.

16

A few days later, I was sitting in the office with a copy of a Missing Persons bulletin in front of me. It was difficult to give it my full attention because my thoughts kept wandering to the delectable person of Mike Blair, Society Editor, Monkton City Globe. She'd scooped the whole coast over the Hoskins Sanatorium fire, and subsequent events, and all due to a few telephone calls from a certain 'well-known private investigator' as the stories had it. More than once, she'd made a point of telling me how much in my debt she was, and I was reflecting on this satisfactory situation when Florence Digby buzzed.

'I have a Mr Swift here, from Federated National Insurers.'

I didn't want to talk to any insurance salesman, but in my business you turn nobody away. It might be a job, and I was already out of pocket through having to pay Sam Thompson's tab on the Rivers thing.

'I'll see him right away.'

He came in almost at a run, a small sharp-featured man with a thatch of white hair which was not about to be bullied by any brush.

'Please take a seat, Mr Swift.'

'Thank you.'

He kept the black leather zip-case on his knees.

'Your secretary told you I was from F.N.I.' he said, in a clipped, precise voice. 'Does it mean anything to you?'

'I try to keep in touch with the insurance world,' I hedged, 'but I don't believe — '

'Perfectly all right. We seek no publicity. The big companies formed F.N.I. a few years back for the protection of their mutual interests. We are not in the insurance business proper, that is to say we sell no policies, or any of the routine matters. You might say we are kind of watchdog organisation.'

All I could do was to look interested. Mr Swift wasn't going to come to the point until he was quite ready.

'If we take just one of the big risks, fire. Have you any idea of how much money changes hands in a twelvemonth, on the grounds of fire alone?'

No I hadn't. But I had to make an offer.

'Millions, I would imagine.'

Mr Swift wasn't given to a lot of smiling, but for me he made an exception.

'Not quite correct, I'm afraid. Hundreds of millions, Mr Preston. Hundreds of millions. Naturally, the companies are very vigilant, with so much money involved.'

Naturally.

'One of the large member companies was at risk in a recent fire, to the tune of six hundred thousand dollars. I am referring of course to the Hoskins Sanatorium.'

I'd been less than just to Mr Swift. He was really a very interesting guy to listen to. And I could make a contribution.

'I knew about that.'

'Yes. Well what you may not know, is

that as a result of a thorough investigation, which followed charges laid by you, it has transpired that the fire was not the unfortunate accident it seemed at the outset. Arson, Mr Preston, arson. The company will not be called upon to meet those charges.'

'Well fine, that's good to know.'

'Better than you realise, I think. In such matters F.N.I. are called in to investigate the circumstances. I have been doing precisely that for the past several days. As a result, I was able to make a recommendation. That recommendation was approved, and so, here I am.'

I nodded encouragingly. He yanked at the zip on the flat case, and poked around inside.

'I have been authorised to pay you a recovering fee. This is calculated on one per cent of the gross. In short sir, I am to present you with a certified cheque for six thousand dollars.'

And that's what he did. I looked at it, afraid it might disappear. Then I mumbled some kind of thanks. Mr Swift zipped up his case, shook me by the hand, and went away.

Six thousand.

I folded the Missing Persons sheet and pushed it away. My hand came back holding the telephone. I was dialling Mike Blair's number. It was time I went into the debt-collecting business.

While I waited for an answer, I lit an Old Favourite. The flame from the lighter was large in front of my face. I remembered those other flames licking, destroying the canvas of Judith Harvey Rivers. Searing at it, till nothing remained but a blackened outline inside the heavy gold frame. I grinned sadly at the thought. In a way the whole thing had been a frame from the outset.

A beautiful golden frame.

THE END

Other titles in the
Linford Mystery Library:

DEATH SQUAD

Basil Copper

Lost in a fog on National Forest terrain, Mike Faraday, the laconic L.A. private investigator, hears shots. A dying man staggers out of the bushes. Paul Dorn, a brilliant criminal lawyer, is quite dead when Mike gets to him. So how could he be killed again in a police shoot-out in L.A. the same night? The terrifying mystery into which Faraday is plunged convinces him that a police death squad is involved. The problem is solved only in the final, lethal shoot-out.

DEAD RECKONING

George Douglas

After a large-scale post office robbery, expert peterman Edgar Mulley's fingerprints are found on a safe and he lands in jail. The money has never been recovered, and three years later Mulley makes a successful break for freedom. The North Central Regional Crime Squad lands the case when a 'grasser' gets information to them. But before Chief Superintendent Hallam and Inspector 'Jack' Spratt can interrogate the informer, he is found dead. Then, a second mysterious death occurs . . .